Fic
Mar   Marino, Jan.
        For the love of Pete

DATE DUE		
OCT 15 1998		
OCT 26 1998		
NOV 2 2 1998		
SEP 28 2001		
MAR 27 2002		
JAN 24 2003		
FEB 13 2003		

        For the Love of
        Pete
Quiz 10117
        Marino, Jan   4.4
        Points: 6 Lvl:

GAYLORD M2

For the Love of Pete

For the Love of Pete

A NOVEL BY JAN MARINO

Little, Brown and Company

BOSTON   NEW YORK   TORONTO   LONDON

19904100

14.95

W88

5/1/98

First Edition

"The Road Goes Ever On," from *The Hobbit,* by J. R. R. Tolkien, copyright © 1966 by J. R. R. Tolkien, is reprinted by permission of Allen & Unwin Publishers Ltd. and Houghton Mifflin Company.

Library of Congress Cataloging-in-Publication Data

Marino, Jan.
    For the love of Pete : a novel / by Jan Marino. — 1st ed.
       p.   cm.
    Summary: When her grandmother moves into a nursing home, twelve-year-old Phoebe sets out in the old family car with three of Gram's servants, on a search for the father who abandoned her at birth.
    ISBN 0-316-54627-5
    [1. Household employees — Fiction.   2. Fathers and daughters — Fiction.]   I. Title.
PZ7.M33884Fo   1993
[Fic] — dc20   92-36465

10 9 8 7 6 5 4 3 2

RRD-VA

Published simultaneously in Canada
by Little, Brown & Company (Canada) Limited

Printed in the United States of America

For my mother, Helen Brown Rejo,
and my father, Ernest D. Rejo,
with love

Acknowledgments

With deep gratitude and affection to Stephanie Owens Lurie, who was there at the beginning, and to Ellen Conford, who made the beginning possible.

A special thank you to St. Ignatius Retreat House, The Hermitage, and Long Island University, C. W. Post Campus, for providing me quiet places.

And a very special thank you to my husband, Len, for providing. . . .

Roads go ever ever on,
Over rock and under tree,
By caves where never sun has shone,
By streams that never find the sea;
Over snow by winter sown,
And through the merry flowers of June,
Over grass and over stone,
And under mountains in the moon.

Roads go ever ever on
Under cloud and under star,
Yet feet that wandering have gone
Turn at last to home afar . . .

J. R. R. Tolkien,
"The Road Goes Ever On," from The Hobbit

Prologue

The summer I turned twelve, I left my grandmother and the home I'd always known and set off to find my father, a man I'd never met. There were four of us on that journey. Bertie and Bishopp and Billy and I.

We traveled from Lubelle County, Georgia, to Okawala, Virginia. Then two of us, Bishopp and I, made our way to Sadler's Island off the coast of Maine.

We drove through small towns, stopping to rest along the way in sad little motels, or huddled in our car, the moonlight our lamp; bounced along dirt roads in a borrowed old pickup truck; picnicked in meadows where cows grazed and bulls ran wild; fished in ponds where fish refused to bite.

So many things happened along the way. But what will always stay with me is the dream I often dreamed when sleep came.

I am in a field of dandelions. Bishopp and Bertie and Billy are with me. My father waits in the clearing. The sun is bright, so bright, he squints to find me. He waves. I stoop to pick some flowers and run to where he waits. He gathers me into his arms, the flowers spilling all over us. Then, from nowhere, rain begins to fall. I tumble from my father's arms. The sun becomes the moon and the flowers burst into great fluffy balls of silver seeds. A wind comes and whirls the seeds around and around, blinding me. I call out, first to Bishopp and then to my father. But they don't answer. I call to Bertie and Billy. Again and again, I call out, but the wind carries my voice away.

PART ONE

❧

Lubelle County

Moving Day

1

$\mathcal{U}$p until my ninth birthday, I believed that somewhere inside my grandmother's grand piano lived a real live person named A. Bosendorfer. Oh, I'd seen lots of pianos, pianos that just sat in the corner of a music room, or a drawing room, or any room for that matter, patiently waiting for somebody to wander over, sit directly in front of middle C, and play. But somehow I knew my grandmother's piano did more than that. The piano talked to her, telling Gram what room he wanted to inhabit next. Gram would call Bishopp and Bertie from whatever they happened to be doing, and off A. Bosendorfer would go.

"A. Bosendorfer needs air and space," my grandmother would say. "He is tired of being cooped up in the music room." She would pat Bosendorfer. "You want to be put back into the dining room, don't you?" Without waiting for an answer, she would say, "He does. And by the window."

Bishopp would swing me up on top of Bosendorfer, where I would sit, tall and still like a bust of Beethoven, while Bishopp and Bertie grunted and groaned Bosendorfer into his new niche.

Gram would stand in her dressing gown, her faded red hair frizzed out around her thin, pale face, ordering Bertie and Bishopp about. "Careful now. Don't bang his sides. No, no, no, not that window. The window that looks out over the rose garden."

Bertie and Bishopp would push until A. Bosendorfer was placed exactly where Gram said he wanted to be. "There now," she would say, patting and stroking the keys. "Are you happy?" She would tilt her head, flutter her powdery-blue eyelids, and then announce, "He says he's very happy." She would turn to Bishopp and Bertie and say, "He says thank you."

Then she would smile at me. "And to you, my sweet, sweet buttercup, he says you are a bit heavier than you were the day he moved up to my bedroom."

That had been an awful day. Bishopp had to call a moving company to move A. Bosendorfer out to the front garden and then hoist him up to the terrace outside Gram's bedroom and into her room. The moving men didn't understand that it wasn't Gram who wanted A. Bosendorfer moved, and when I tried to explain it to them, they just shook their heads, looked over at Gram, and muttered, "Crazy old bird."

What did the moving men know? Moving A. Bosendorfer day was usually fun. I loved it. Even though Bishopp and Bertie felt otherwise when they were pushing Bosendorfer around, things changed rapidly when he was in place.

"Tea party time," Gram would announce. Bishopp would set up a tea table under the oak tree while Gram dressed the two of us into something "appropriate for such a grand occasion."

When I was very little, Gram would try to get Bertie and Bishopp to dress in their Sunday best.

"Wear the dress you wore when you made your debut at Tivoli Gardens."

"Livia, I can't get my toe in that old thing," Bertie would say, laying out her tiny sandwiches and sugar cakes.

"And you," Gram would ask Bishopp. "Why don't you put on your tails?"

Bishopp would shake his head and say the tails had flown off with the moths.

When we were all gathered around the table, Bertie would say a little prayer; Gram would ask us all to raise our teacups for a toast. "To Bosendorfer. May he be happy in his new abode forever."

"Amen to that," Bertie and Bishopp would say, and we would begin our feast.

Gram always asked Miss Jean if she'd like to join in, but Miss Jean would just stand next to the tea table, her nurse's uniform as stiff and white as her hair, and mutter something about the propriety of the butler and the cook having tea with the mistress of the house. That was just like Miss Jean, worrying about the propriety of things, always snooping around Bishopp's pantry, then reporting to Gram that Bishopp was slipping. "Shining silver, gleaming like stars, is the mark of a good butler. And the good Lord knows, the only stars around here are the ones in that old monster he keeps in his pantry."

"That old monster" was Bishopp's telescope. Miss Jean was always saying it was a ridiculous piece of equipment and should be thrown out. What Miss Jean didn't realize was that Bishopp's telescope was magic. Through it, I saw swirling dragons and moonlike stars, and the moon's mountains, invisible to my bare eyes. Bishopp knew every star and constellation by name. Pollux and Castor. Capella and Orion.

Miss Jean didn't realize other things about Bishopp. He saw to so many things — the bills that Gram let pile up on the hall table, the flowers that Gram planted and never watered, the old stove that always gave Bertie trouble. And me.

Without him, nothing would be right. I knew that. Gram knew it, too, even though she never came right out and said it.

Bertie knew it, even though she argued with Bishopp over anything and everything. She always told me my mother knew it. And if I had ever met my father, I just know he'd say the same thing.

Most of the days that followed moving Bosendorfer were fun, too. Gram would play Bosendorfer and sing arias — with gusto, as she said. She would la la la la la la la in one octave, and lo lo lo lo lo lo lo in another. But as the days passed, the fun would creep away like the mold that crept down the path leading to the river. Bishopp would go around the house shaking his head.

Bertie would mumble. Miss Jean would sulk. And I would lie in bed those nights listening to Gram banging on Bosendorfer, singing very loud, sometimes until the sun rose and lit up the river beyond the tulip tree. Those nights frightened me.

Eventually Gram hardly slept at all. She would dress in her old costumes, sometimes changing a dozen times a day. In the morning she would be Musetta, at lunchtime Madama Butterfly, and at dinner she would be Tosca.

"I'm readying myself for another world tour," she would say. "OUT! OUT! OUT!" she would shout at the top of her lungs whenever Miss Jean suggested she should rest. "Rest is not what I need. I need practice. Milan is a very difficult audience and I intend to be ready."

She would call Bishopp and ask him over and over, "I'm right about that, aren't I?" Bishopp would nod and tell her of course she was right, his eyes cast down so they would not betray his words, and Gram would happily go back to Bosendorfer.

I knew all about Gram's days on the stage. I had heard the story of her debut at the Milan Opera Company hundreds of times. "Oh, dear child," she would begin, "the stage was filled with roses. All colors. Red. Yellow. White. The fragrance would make my head spin." I would picture my grandmother on the stage, roses up to her ankles. I would see her bending over, scooping up an armful of roses, breathing in their fragrance, taking bow after bow. See the audience stand, hear them stamp their feet and shout to Gram, "Brava. Brava." I would see Gram take her final bow, then back away from the stage lights, her tiny feet crushing the roses, leaving a rainbow of petals at her feet. It was fun to see all that, but when those days ended, I saw and heard other things.

A. Bosendorfer would be shut up tight and covered with a shawl. Gram no longer called me "my little buttercup" or "sweet little bird of my heart." She barely knew me.

She would stay in her bed, her door shut tight. Every morning I would tiptoe into her room, hoping Gram would open her eyes and say good morning. I would wait long, long minutes, then back out of her room and close the door quietly behind me.

Darkness gathered around the house, as though the sun were afraid to enter. The kitchen, where Bishopp and Bertie spent much of their time, was the only room that seemed sunny.

They would busy themselves with their day's work, taking turns bustling in and out of Gram's room. "Have some tea?" Bishopp would ask. He would summon Bertie's brother, Billy Hill, to take Gram for a drive, but Gram refused to leave her bed.

"Ginny Graham sent you some of those cinnamon buns you like so much," Bertie would say. But Gram didn't seem to hear. She didn't even hear Miss Jean say that it was time for Gram to go to "that place. That place where people like her belonged."

On the morning of my ninth birthday Gram went

to "that place" for the first time, and it was on that morning I knew A. Bosendorfer no longer lived in the piano. At first I thought maybe Gram took him with her, leaving just the piano sitting alone in the drawing room, just like any other piano. Still. Silent. Waiting.

But before the morning was over, I knew that the gold lettering spelling out "Bosendorfer" was just the name of a piano company.

Poor Butterfly

2

The morning of my ninth birthday, I woke up with a start. Not because I was excited about finally being nine years old, which I was, but because of the commotion going on in the hall outside my bedroom.

"Call my Livvy," I heard my grandmother say. "She'll tell you my booking agent is making arrangements this very day for me to sail to Milan."

"Easy, now, ma'am," a strange voice said. "You just take it easy."

I heard a scream and then: "YOU, SIR, DON'T LET THEM DO THIS TO ME!"

I leapt out of bed and ran to the hall. "Wait!" I shouted to the strangers making their way down the winding staircase, my grandmother between them. "Wait."

"Get back to your room," Miss Jean called from the bottom of the stairs. "You're nearly naked." She started up the stairs. "Besides, this is no place for a child."

I flew back to my room, yanked my bathrobe from

its hook, wrapped it around me, and raced back to the hall.

Gram was sitting between the strangers, their arms forming a seat for her. Her arms were crossed over her chest and bound with something that looked like a huge white bandage. I almost laughed because she looked like a butterfly whose head was bursting from its cocoon.

"Take me to the dock," she wailed. "Livvy's waiting at the ship."

Bishopp was beside her, stroking her hair. "Livvy will wait."

That frightened me. My mother was dead. Bishopp knew that. My grandmother looked up at him. "She will?"

Bishopp nodded. "She will."

"Are you sure?"

Again he nodded.

My grandmother smiled up at him. "You are very kind, sir. Very kind indeed."

"Why is she calling you 'sir'?" I shouted.

Bishopp kept stroking her hair.

"Will you do me another kindness?" Gram asked.

"My pleasure."

"Inform the maestro —" My grandmother stopped. She sat up straight, thrust her chin out, and said, "That I will be needing a Bosendorfer. Nothing less than a Bosendorfer will do."

"I'll be happy to tell him."

"Oh, my, you are kind." Then she waved her

hand, glanced up at the two men flanking her chair, and said, "Now off to the ship, if you please, gentlemen. A diva is never late."

"Gram!" I shouted, racing down the stairs. "Wait."

Gram turned. "A child," she said, smiling at me. "How dear. There is nothing as dear as a child."

I stood before her. "Don't tease, Gram. It's me. It's —"

She closed her eyes and shook her head. "Don't tell me your name, I know it — Mimi. Oh, how splendid you were at LaScala." Her eyes opened wide. "What's this? Tears? No need for tears, Mimi. Remember how Rodolfo loved you? He held you in his arms long after your dear sweet soul had slipped into eternity." She smiled. "Come now, give Musetta a farewell kiss. The ship is waiting."

"Stop it!" I shouted. "You're Gram and I'm Phoebe —"

Bishopp put his hand on my shoulder. "Your grandmother must leave."

"But she doesn't know me." My eyes burned, my throat tightened. "And it's my birthday."

"I know."

I turned to my grandmother. "Did you forget?"

"Forget? It isn't I who is forgetting. It's all of you."

She looked at Bishopp. "Other than you, sir, this is a congregation of fools. Nobody seems to understand that Livvy is waiting." She smiled at him. "Will you be good enough to tell Carl to bring the car around?"

Carl had been gone since Christmas. Billy Hill drove the car now. "I'm so sorry, Carl," my grandmother had said, "but I simply cannot afford to pay you any longer."

Bishopp nodded and told Gram he'd be happy to get Carl.

"But, Bishopp —" I said, a shiver running through me.

He hushed me with a look.

"While I'm doing that," he said, "these good gentlemen will help you to your car."

Gram beamed. "I shall not forget your kindness, sir."

"Say good-bye to your grandmother," Bishopp said, his voice low and steady. "Quickly, please."

"But —"

"Now."

"But it's my birthday."

"I know," he said gently, "but your grandmother must go."

I looked up and for one tiny minute thought I saw tears in Bishopp's eyes. "Say good-bye," he said one final time. "It's time."

And I did.

Gram didn't ask, but I promised her I'd be good. "I'll practice my flute, and by the time you come home I'll have 'Clair de Lune' memorized, and we can play a duet." I gave her a kiss and whispered, "I'll save you a piece of birthday cake. A big one."

"We're wasting time," one of the men said. He

motioned with his chin to the other man and they floated Gram out of the house and into the early morning fog.

"Bye-bye, everyone," she called back. "I'm off. Off to LaScala." Then she disappeared into the gray mist.

Let the River Run

3

"Hello, hello, hello," Gram called out, blowing kisses to everybody. Billy Hill followed her through the front door, carrying her suitcases.

I'd stopped counting the times that she'd come home from Shady Lawn, but I did know the number of birthdays she'd missed. My ninth. My tenth. My eleventh. And she'd probably miss this year, too.

I stood on the stairs watching Bishopp help Gram take off her coat. She looked so small, as though her dress hung from a hanger and not Gram. "It's good to have you home again, Mrs.," Bishopp said, smiling down at her.

She turned to him and touched his face, quickly. "Oh, Bish, it is so lovely to be home again."

She looked around, and when she saw me standing on the stairs she said, "Oh, sweet little bird of my heart, how you've grown since I've been gone."

I raced down the stairs and into her open arms. She gathered me in and squeezed me hard. She took my face in her hands and smiled. "Oh, my, my," she said, "I'm really home."

She looked over at Bertie and blew her a kiss. "What have you been feeding my sweet little wren?"

Bertie smiled, all decked out in cook's uniform. "I've fixed your favorite. Veal, nice and tender." Bishopp stood beside Bertie wearing his creamy-white linen jacket and skinny black tie, all butler-like. Three places were set in the dining room: Gram's. Miss Jean's. And mine. I didn't like those changes that came with Gram's homecoming, the changes Miss Jean instituted: Bertie stuffed into a black uniform; Bishopp all gussied up; Miss Jean back in residence; Bertie and Bishopp in the kitchen eating alone. I hated that most.

When Gram was gone I spent a lot of time in the kitchen, watching Bertie fuss with supper, listening to the two of them bickering over some little thing. And long after supper, after Bertie was asleep and sleep wouldn't come to me, I would creep downstairs to the pantry where Bishopp most always was. Together we would search the night sky until we came upon Perseus or Fishes. Then I would ask Bishopp to find Polaris, the star he told me never changes its place in the sky. I would take Bishopp's hand and we would both wish Gram home. I knew Bishopp really didn't believe in wishing, but he always wished her home with me.

"Why does Miss Jean have to come back?" I whispered to Bishopp when my grandmother started upstairs, Miss Jean behind her, fussing about the way Billy

Hill walked too close behind her, the way he banged Gram's suitcases into the railing.

"Because your grandmother is in need of nursing care."

"But Gram doesn't like her. She's such a snob, and she's got nothing to be snobby about."

"Watch that, Miss Phoebe," Bishopp whispered.

"See? That's what I mean. Just because Miss Jean is back, I've got to be Miss Phoebe again."

"Good manners dictate that we not upset people unnecessarily," Bishopp said. "And we all know how upsettable Miss Jean is."

"Good manners dictate that you're nice to every-body, and Miss Jean's only nice when she thinks some-body is important."

Bishopp sighed. "We can't change Miss Jean, so I suggest you get yourself used to being Miss Phoebe again."

"I know for a fact Gram doesn't like it when you call me 'Miss Phoebe,' and she hates it when you call her 'The Mrs.' " I put my hand on Bishopp's arm. "She called you 'Bish.' "

"That will be enough, Miss Phoebe."

I sighed a long sigh. "In the kitchen, too?"

"The kitchen, too."

"Phoebe, my love," Gram called. "Come. I've so much to tell you."

Bishopp motioned and I followed Billy up the stairs. Gram oohed and aahed at everything she passed.

When she got to the upstairs hall, she went over to the mirror next to my room and looked at herself. She fluffed out her hair, then inspected her teeth. "Billy," she said, "we'll be visiting with Dr. Sperling first thing tomorrow." She smiled a false smile at herself. "Teeth are important and I intend to keep mine until I breathe my last."

Miss Jean kept prodding Gram down to her room. That was another thing about Miss Jean that I hated, always shuffling Gram off to her room, trying to keep her quiet and rested when Gram didn't want to be quiet and rested at all.

When Miss Jean first came, I used to tell Bertie that more than anything I wanted to find a magic powder to sprinkle on Miss Jean, to make her smaller and smaller, until she was so small I could stuff her into a bottle, bring it down to the river, and let her float downstream until the bottle disappeared. But now that I was older, I knew that if Miss Jean disappeared, so would Gram.

"Where is my buttercup," Gram sang,

> *sweet little buttercup,*
> *dear little buttercup, mine . . .*

"Right behind you, Gram."

"Miz Olivia, you know what Doctor said. You need rest and quiet."

"Rest and quiet be damned. I've had enough of that. I need my sweet little bird. And my music. That's what I need."

I ran past Billy. "You'll never guess what I did on my flute the other day."

"What, my precious?"

"I held high C so long Miss Minnow said it was the longest high C in the history of the Sasha Minnow School of Classical Music." I put my arm around Gram's waist. "She said I was her best student."

"Of course you are. And why wouldn't you be? You have musical genes bursting and bubbling inside you. Lots and lots of them. Why, your mother was better than I at Bosendorfer."

Gram never, ever spoke of my father, but once, a long time ago, I heard Bertie say that my father played the harp like an angel.

"Miz Olivia," Miss Jean said, taking Gram's arm, "remember what Doctor said." Gram waved her away.

"Doctor be damned, too." She smiled at me. "We shall have music. A concert. And tea. And sandwiches. And, of course, dear, sweet Bertie's sugar cakes."

"You need rest."

"Where's Bosendorfer, sweet thing?"

"Where you left him, Gram."

"Where was that?"

"In your room. Don't you remember?"

"I will not be part of this," Miss Jean said.

"Nor should you be. This is just our concert. Right, my sweet? Just yours and mine."

For a while, it was. Gram played Bosendorfer. I played my flute. Tea parties with Bertie and Bishopp, Miss Jean complaining all the while.

And then, as before, Gram would begin to change over time. She played sad, dark music on Bosendorfer, far into the night. She refused to eat breakfast, even Ginny Graham's cinnamon buns. Bishopp and I picked her favorite blackberries, but she didn't want them. She stayed in her nightgown all day, even though Bertie pleaded with her to dress, so as not to catch cold. Miss Jean threatened to take her back to Shady Lawn. But Gram didn't seem to hear anything but Bosendorfer.

One morning before the sun came up, a loud crash came from Gram's room. I leapt out of bed and ran to her room. Gram's bed hadn't been slept in, and her bedside lamp was on the floor, its glass shade shattered. Bosendorfer was shut tight, his shawl wrapped around him.

The room was very cold, so I went to the window to close it, and when I did, I saw my grandmother through the mist. She was standing at the edge of the river. Naked. I turned and pulled the shawl from Bosendorfer and ran down the stairs, screaming, "Bishopp! Bishopp! Help me."

By the time I got to the back door, he was there. He clutched my hand and the two of us raced out of the house and toward the river. Gram was walking into the water, her arms raised over her head.

"Olivia!" Bishopp shouted. "Stop! Stop!" Gram kept walking, and by the time we got to the river's edge, all I could see of her were her fingers.

Without stopping to take off his shoes, Bishopp dived into the water and swam out to Gram. When he got to her, she struggled with him, but he held her fast and swam back to where I stood. He carried her in his arms as though she were a baby and told me to wrap the shawl around her. "Olivia. Olivia," he murmured. Gram stared straight ahead, a tiny smile on her lips.

"They have been waiting too long," she said. "Far too long."

A shiver raced up my spine. I shook her out-stretched arm. "Gram. Gram. Look at me. I'm here. Look at me."

But she didn't.

"Come, Phoebe," Bishopp said, his voice barely above a whisper, "let's get her back."

We headed toward the house, the squishing sound from Bishopp's shoes breaking the morning stillness. Hot tears filled my eyes, blurring everything around me. I reached out and held on to Bishopp's jacket and let him lead me home.

While Gram was readied and helped into the car, I sat alone in her bedroom, staring at Bosendorfer, mute in the corner, and trying to push away the feeling that this was Gram's last trip to Shady Lawn. That there was to be no homecoming ever again.

Turn of the Tide

4

"Today's goin' down in the annals of weather history, folks." Joe Cudjoe's voice floated out from Bertie's ancient Philco radio, through the kitchen window, and over to the porch swing where I sat. "You folks be sure to wear your coolest today," WBZL's singing weatherman went on to say, " 'cause it's gonna be one u-u-uugly day. Temperature's promisin' to get up as high as one hundred and five, with matchin' humidity."

Bertie came out onto the porch, fanning herself with the bottom of her apron. "I'm telling you something," she said, settling herself beside me. "Soon as I get me some extra cash I'm going to buy me a big, wide fan." She wiped her face with her apron. "Then I'm going to sit me down by the river with a tall, cold glass of tea in one hand, my fan in the other, and have me a nice, cool afternoon." She smiled down at me. "You know what I'm saying?"

I was just about to tell Bertie that I'd seen a huge fan belonging to Gram, one that she'd used in some big opera, when Miss Jean's nephew pulled into the driveway and Miss Jean stepped out of the car. "You better get a move on if you think you're going to visit your grandmother," she said, as she walked across the porch. "Visiting hours for children start at noon. Sharp." She squared her nurse's cap on her head and opened the door to the kitchen.

Bertie nudged me and whispered, "I wish that hat of hers had a motor set on top. One that would fly her around like that old Mary Poppins person. Only I'd like the hat to forget where it came from." I started to laugh, then Bertie started up.

Miss Jean must have heard us because she stuck her head out the kitchen window and said, "Are you hearing me?"

"Yes," I said, "we are hearing you."

"Bertie," Miss Jean called. "Remember now that Miz Howland would like you and Bishopp to come later on in the day. She's got something to discuss with the two of you."

"I know. I know," Bertie said. "But Bishopp and I'll be coming along with you and Miss Phoebe. Takes too long coming and going, specially when Billy's got a mess of errands he's got to tend to."

Miss Jean pulled her head and her hat back through the window.

It wasn't Gram's idea for Bertie and Bishopp to come later, we all knew that. Miss Jean just liked to give orders.

Bertie sighed and heaved herself from the swing.

"Come on, sugar babe, there's no use arguing with that lady. We best get ourselves ready, heat and all."

I put my arm around Bertie and the two of us went back into the house. The breakfast dishes were still piled on the table, so I helped Bertie clean up, then I put on my Shady Lawn Rest Home dress, sat in my room until I was called, and filed into Gram's car with all the rest. Billy Hill started the motor, and off we went.

I hated to go to Shady Lawn, especially on the days when Gram didn't know who I was. On those days, she'd call me Musetta or Mimi, or she'd be Mimi and she'd look at Bishopp and say, *"Che gelida manina . . ."* Bishopp told me those were the words Mimi spoke on her deathbed, words that Rodolfo had spoken to Mimi when they fell in love. He told me that I shouldn't be sad when Gram did that. He told me when people were ill they sometimes lived in the past, where they were happy, because at times the present was too painful.

There were other things at Shady Lawn that made me sad. Like the viewing room, where they showed old movies. Old people sitting in chairs, heads drooping, not looking at the screen, some of them smiling as I passed, me smiling back, wondering why they smiled, wondering why I smiled back when I really wanted to cry.

When we got to Shady Lawn, Gram wasn't finished with her breakfast. Bishopp said he had something to attend to in the business office; the rest of us waited in the dayroom. Miss Maude Eckman, as always, was sitting in her wheelchair, holding the same shabby piece of paper that Bishopp told me was a letter from her nephew in California. Miss Eckman's cloud-like hair was tied up on top with a pink bow. Like a baby. I sat there for a long while, looking at that bow, feeling angry, so angry that I got up and told one of the nurses they should take the bow out of her hair. "She looks silly," I said, and ran from the dayroom down to the solarium.

Miss Jean followed me, telling me that this was the reason Shady Lawn didn't want children coming and going. "What business is it of yours if the staff chooses to dress up one of their charges? You just tend to your own business, or I'll see to it that you don't get to visit your grandmother again."

"You'll see to nothing," said Bertie, bustling into the solarium. She came over to me. "It's all right. I know what's bothering you. It bothers me, too."

She turned to Miss Jean, her voice a loud whisper. "You don't think this child is feeling so many feelings, she doesn't know where she's at? You got any idea about what's going on inside her?" Miss Jean started to say something, but Bertie interrupted. "This poor baby is thinking about her grammy, and she's scared."

"She's overdramatizing," Miss Jean said. "That's her problem." She glared at me. "You stop this carrying on."

"*You* stop carrying on," Bertie said. "You've got no more feelings in you than that piece of pink ribbon sitting on top of that poor old lady's head."

Bertie put her arm around me and headed me toward the door. "We'll get us a nice cool drink of tea," she said. "That'll make things better."

It didn't, and when it was time to see Gram, Bertie told me that I should wait a bit before visiting with her. "You calm yourself down, sugar babe. Then come on out to the veranda and we'll have a real nice visit. They tell me your grammy's more like herself today than she's been in a long time."

I sat in the commissary for a while, calming myself as best I could, and then started over to where Gram was waiting.

I was just about to round the corner to the veranda when I heard Bishopp's voice. ". . . you ask us to take her, after all these years of forbidding us to speak of him?"

Gram said something I couldn't hear.

"What papers?" Bishopp asked.

Gram said something else I couldn't hear, and then, "I put . . . I put . . . ," her voice breaking off.

I peered around until I could see them.

Bishopp stood in front of Gram. "Try to remember."

Again Gram said something I couldn't hear. Then she closed her eyes, her head dropped forward. "Oh, God," she cried, "what did I do?"

Bishopp leaned over and took her hand.

"It was wrong," she said.

"What was wrong?" Bishopp said.

Gram just stared ahead.

"It *was* wrong," Gram wailed. "Oh, dear God, help me." She started to cry. "What was I to do? She was all I had. She was all that was left." She tried to get up from where she sat, then slumped down. She looked up at Bishopp, then at Bertie. "He didn't know. She was my heart." She reached out for Bertie's hand.

"Who didn't know?"

Gram started to cry.

Bertie leaned over and held her. "Hush. Hush." She rocked Gram back and forth. Bertie looked over at Bishopp. "You remember the summer Ginny Graham was with us? I seem to recollect her trying to help Livia sort through all kinds of papers. It was the summer Phoebe broke her leg —"

"Where *is* Phoebe?" Bishopp asked Bertie. "You said she was following right along after you."

I backed away from the corner, waited a few seconds, then ran around to the veranda. "Gram," I called. "I'm here."

She looked at me and held out her arms. "Oh, my dear, dear child," she said. "My dear, sweet, darling child."

She hugged me, then took my hands in hers and said, "Oh, Livvy, Livvy —"

"I'm not Livvy," I said, pulling back from her. "I'm Phoebe —"

"These good people will take care of you, Livvy."

She reached out and took my hands again, tears running down her cheeks.

"Oh, please, Gram, please," I said, squeezing her hands, "I'm not my mother."

She smiled a weak smile.

"She's very tired, Phoebe," Bishopp said, his voice gentle. He put his arm around me. "I think it's time to leave."

But I held on to Gram's hands until the head nurse came out to the veranda and said visiting hours were over for children. I hugged her hard and told her how much I loved her. She hugged me back, and whispered, "One day soon, my sweet, you'll fly away."

I Heard It Through the Grapevine

5

*O*n the drive back home, I sat squeezed between Bertie and Miss Jean. Bertie kept fanning herself with her handkerchief; Miss Jean kept asking me to sit still; Bishopp sat cool and erect next to Billy.

Just before we got to where Miss Jean lived, Bertie asked Billy to stop at the supermarket. "We need milk and bread for supper," she said.

As soon as Billy went into the market, Miss Jean leaned over toward Bishopp. "When do you all plan on carrying out Miz Howland's desires?" She motioned back toward me. "Somebody is definitely not going to like it. Especially closing up the house and all."

"Closing up what house?" I said.

Bishopp shook his head, then turned and gave Miss Jean a nasty look.

"Sorry," Miss Jean said.

"Did you mean our house?" I said, wiggling my way to the edge of the seat.

Miss Jean shrugged. "Just a thought, what with finances being what they are." She pulled herself from where she was sitting and put her hand on the door handle. "I'm so close to home, I think I'll walk the rest of the way." She got out of the car, then poked her head in the window. "See that Billy has my personals back to me by Friday. I'm leaving for Richmond come the end of July."

All the way home, I thought about what she'd said. I knew Bishopp always worried about money and that Gram didn't have nearly as much as she used to, but why would he close up our house? Where would we go? What would we do?

Bertie had to poke me twice when it was time to help her out of the car. She asked me to give her a hand with supper, but I told her I wasn't feeling so good. The truth was, I couldn't stop thinking about what Miss Jean had said. The way Bishopp had looked at her. The way she'd said she was sorry. That wasn't like her. She was the one who was always saying Gram should "sell this old mess."

I went up to my room and sat on the edge of my bed.

Miss Jean was right for once. Money was a problem. Bishopp always paid the bills; Gram never had. "I hate figures," she always said. But lately, it took him a long time to figure things out. He'd sit at the kitchen table, adding and subtracting, and once I heard him tell Bertie she'd have to wait for her shopping money.

Then I remembered what Miss Jean had said about doing as Gram wished and that somebody wouldn't like it. And what I overheard Bishopp say to Gram about taking somebody someplace. *Take her,* he had said. "Take who, where?" I said out loud. I decided to ask.

I bolted from my bed and headed downstairs, but stopped midway. The *her* Bishopp was talking about, the *her* they were taking someplace, had to be me. I walked slowly back up the stairs and into my room, closing the door behind me.

What did Bishopp say after that? Something about Gram forbidding them to talk about . . . him. I sat down hard on the bed. "The him is my father," I said. "Gram wants them to take me to my father."

Well, I'm not going. I'm staying here with Bishopp and Bertie and Billy. Where I belong. Near Gram. Not with some father who never even came to see me, never even wanted me. "I'm not some . . . some . . . some old baby that can be plunked down on somebody's doorstep," I said, then put my hand over my mouth when I heard somebody coming up the stairs.

"Phoebe," Bertie called, "you all right?"

I opened the door. She was standing on the landing. "I'm fine," I said.

"Talking to yourself again?"

I shrugged. "I guess."

"Well, tell yourself to set the table." She started back downstairs. "No rush. Supper won't be ready for a while."

My stomach really felt sick now. How could Gram want me to be with him? She always told me he never could take care of me. Why would he want me now? Now that I could take care of myself.

I took off my Shady Lawn dress, put on some shorts and a top, and went down the back stairs, through the pantry, and into the kitchen. Bertie wasn't there; neither was Bishopp.

I was just about to set the table when I heard Bishopp's voice coming from the front hall.

"Yes, I'm sure that's how the name is spelled. Would you give it another look, please?"

I peered into the hall. Bishopp was on the telephone, Bertie beside him.

"Is there any way I can obtain an unlisted number?" He shook his head. "Perhaps an address?" Again he shook his head. "Thank you anyway."

He put the receiver down and turned to Bertie. "Livia has got to think harder." He sighed a long, sad sigh. "Or we've got to come up with those papers."

I backed away until I reached the stairs in Bishopp's pantry. "Not if I find them first," I whispered as I tiptoed back up the steps.

I ran across the hall and back down the front stairs and as though I hadn't heard anything said, "I'm going to set the table now. Supper must be almost ready."

As soon as I had helped Bertie clear up the kitchen, I excused myself and went back up to my room. I waited until I heard the creak of the back porch swing. I knew it was Bertie. I went to the back stairs and crept midway down. I could see Bishopp at the kitchen table, studying what looked like a map.

I got a flashlight from the upstairs linen closet, stuffed it in my pocket, and made my way up to the attic. The only light came from a tiny window at the far end, but it was enough for me to see millions of spiderwebs hanging everywhere. They caught in my hair and swept across my face. I held my hand over my nose so I wouldn't sneeze as the dust from old trunks and suitcases floated around me.

Shining the flashlight, I went through boxes and shopping bags. At the bottom of one, I found old pictures of Gram and clippings from her days on the stage of the Milan Opera Company. A young Gram, so beautiful, always receiving praise from the critics. And then an older Gram, tired looking, with not so much praise, and many of the reviews torn away.

There were three clippings about Billy Hill, telling how he had single-handedly rescued a platoon from behind enemy lines in Vietnam when the lieutenant in charge had been killed. How he had lost an arm in the rescue.

But no papers.

I crawled under the eaves and aimed the flashlight behind one of the chimneys. A family of mice had made a nest in the far corner, and when the last of them scurried off, I shined the light farther into the eaves, and there it was. The fan. It was sitting on top of a huge trunk. As I inched my way over, a splinter pierced my knee. I kept going.

A string hung from a light above the trunk. I lit the light, lifted the trunk's cover, and there, I was sure, were the papers Bertie and Bishopp would be looking for. Letters and notebooks. More clippings. I scooped them out and was just about to close the trunk when I saw a long piece of paper, rolled and wrapped with pink ribbon, tucked in the trunk's cover. I slipped the ribbon from it and unrolled the paper. It was my birth certificate. When I read it, I fell back against the chimney to catch my breath.

"Dominique Phoebe Howland Fiore," I whispered. "Father: Dominic Paul Fiore. Mother: Olivia Phoebe Howland."

I carefully put everything in a shopping bag, crawled out from the eaves, and slipped back down to my room.

Spreading the papers on my bed, I went through each one. From one clipping I learned that my father was a concert harpist who had accompanied Gram when she sang in London. I found only one picture of him, sitting at the harp, his back to the camera, Gram facing it. The caption under it read: "Olivia Stanton Howland and her new accompanist, Dominic Fiore. Fiore's brilliant performances have in large measure contributed to Stanton Howland's successful comeback." It was dated June 1963. I looked at it for a long time, knowing now where my dark hair came from.

I found two letters from my father. One from San Francisco dated September 1972, telling Gram he had finally gotten himself together and was able to resume his life. He said he regretted ever leaving my mother and that he understood Gram's reaction when he visited her.

> *I was a poor excuse for a husband, leaving her for even one day when she was pregnant with my child. But I had no way of knowing the child would come so early, and the end so quickly. Please believe that, Olivia. Believe, too, that I loved and still love Livvy, as I will never love another.*

There was another letter. It was postmarked Sadler's Island, Maine. He said he was doing very well, and should she ever need anything, anything at all, he could be reached through the address on the back of the envelope. "You were, after all, the mother of my Livvy and the grandmother of our child."

When I finished, I gathered up everything and put it in my bottom drawer. The air was thick, my room hot and sticky. I opened the fan wide, shook the dust from it, and brought it out to the porch.

"Well, look at that," Bertie said, smiling. "Just what I've always wanted. A big, wide fan."

She flipped it open and fanned herself. "Where'd you get this, Phoebe?"

I sat down and with my feet planted on the floor, pushed the swing back, lifted my feet, and let the swing go. A soft, sweet breeze cooled my cheeks, then brushed the back of my neck. When the swing came to a stop, I turned to Bertie and said, "My real name is Dominique. Did you know that?"

The smile left Bertie's face. She put the fan down, put her arm around me, nodded slowly, and said, "So now you know." Then she pushed the swing hard and we swung back and forth.

A hundred hours seemed to pass before Bertie spoke again. "I'm glad," she said. "I surely am."

Another hundred hours passed before I spoke. "We're not going," I said. "We can't."

"What are you saying?"

"We're not leaving here. Not leaving Gram. We can stay. I've thought of a way."

"What are you talking about?"

"You remember that picture we saw at Shady Lawn? The one where they turned that big old house into an inn?"

She nodded.

"They made a lot of money."

"I seem to recall they had some big movie stars there," Bertie said. "Singers and dancers."

"I'll help you cook, and Billy can set chairs out on the lawn, so people can sit and watch the sunset —"

"Phoebe, honey —"

"Gram could sit out there, too, same as she sits up at Shady Lawn. Bishopp can serve tea and Billy can take people boating on the river —"

Bertie tried to say something, but I went right on. "We'll put a sign by the road so when people travel by —"

"Traveling where? This place is a dead end —"

"Then we'll put an ad in the paper. Like Mr. Henson did when he wanted to rent out his barn."

"Mr. Henson rented his barn to Miz Garrett's cows. Cows. Not visiting people. Folks don't come to Lubelle County on a whim."

"We can sell your preserves. Baskets of blackberries. There are lots of ways —"

"Phoebe, honey," Bertie said, shaking her head. "It's just not going to happen."

I got up and walked from the porch and toward the river. "Well, we're not leaving here," I said, my voice too low for Bertie to hear. "Ever."

Bring Your Sorrows
to the Riverside

6

"*I* was sure I'd find you here," Bishopp said, settling himself beside me. "We need to talk, don't we?"

I tugged at a stubborn piece of eelgrass and shrugged, afraid if I spoke, the tears that had been building up would let go.

He put his hand on mine and tugged along with me until the grass came loose, landing us both backward onto the cool, damp ground.

Bishopp laughed out loud. "Well," he said, "we're in the proper position to make another search for Hercules."

I sat up and started to say I didn't want to, but he kept on talking.

"Such a contrast, Hercules. As a Greek hero he's strong, shines brighter than Polaris. But as a constellation he's weak; his stars lack brilliance." He put his hands in back of his head and stared up at the sky. "And yet, if one looks hard enough, he's there."

I started to get up, but he reached out and took my arm. "There, Phoebe," he said, raising my arm toward the sky. "There he is."

I pulled my arm back. "I don't care about him! I don't care about anything. I care about me. About me and what's going to happen.

"You think I don't know what's going on? Well, I do, and I'm not going. And I don't want to hear anything about my father. Because it's not going to happen."

"Phoebe —"

"I'm not going to live with him even for a day and nobody can make me." I got up fast, so fast, my foot slipped and I fell. The tears broke loose.

I cried long and hard, not for my skinned knees or the blood trickling from my nose. Bishopp didn't try to stop me. He wiped my face with his handkerchief, brushed the hair from my face, and waited until I cried myself out.

"It's not fair," I said, finally, my voice shaking.

"I know, Phoebe, life does seem that way at times. For all of us. Even for old Hercules up there." He took his jacket off and put it around my shoulders. "Let's go up to the porch," he said. "You'll catch your death here."

We sat on the porch step. Sounds from Bertie's kitchen drifted out. Cicadas chirped. And an owl hooted in the distance. Bishopp started to talk, but I wasn't listening. I was thinking about my father.

I used to wonder where he was and if he would ever come to see me again. From the time I was very little, Gram told me he was very sick. "He is simply not able to care for you," she would say, hugging me close. "But Gram will always be here." Then, as always, she would tell me how much she loved me, how nobody could ever love me as she did, and it would all end with kisses and hugs.

I used to believe Gram, but when I got to be about seven or so, I knew my father just didn't want me. I'd hear bits and pieces of conversation, like Gram telling Bishopp about my father being "too busy doing things decent people wouldn't dream of doing to take care of his child." And once, although Gram denied she said it, I heard her tell Bertie that when he'd visited me as a baby, "It had never entered that man's mind that the child belonged with her father."

Whenever I asked Gram about him, she'd get a sudden headache or a dizzy spell. If I asked Bishopp or Bertie, they always remembered something they'd forgotten to do and off they'd go. So I imagined him myself. Imagined meeting him. Imagined loving him. Imagined him loving me. But now everything was different.

"Phoebe," Bishopp said, cupping my chin in his hand, "you're not listening."

I didn't want to hear what he was saying, but he held my face close to his and said, "Your grandmother is very ill. You know that." He took a deep breath and let it out slowly. "And somehow you've come to the

conclusion that she wants you to be with your father."
He took his hand from my face. "You're right."

I felt as though somebody had punched me in the chest. "But he doesn't want me. She knows that. He never wanted me."

"People change."

"I won't. I'm not leaving here. I'm staying with you, and Bertie, just like always."

Bishopp sighed a heavy sigh. "Phoebe, there are problems —"

"I know. Money. But we can make enough money if we —"

He nodded. "I heard. The inn."

"We can do it."

"We're managing to keep your grandmother where she has to be, and we'll continue to do so, but there simply is no money to turn this house into an inn. Even if there were, I'll be sixty-five next summer, and Bertie's close to sixty. You can see how her arthritis is slowing her down —"

"Billy's not old, and I could help."

He shook his head. "Phoebe, you need to be with —"

"Don't talk like that," I sobbed. "I don't want to go."

"Nor do I. I've been with your grandmother a long time. Bertie longer. But circumstances are such that we have little choice." He put his arm around me. "You're a child. You need a younger parent —"

"No!" I shouted, shaking my head. "No. No. No. I'm staying here."

"Phoebe, listen to me, please. It's not possible for us to continue like this.

"It's difficult for all of us. Bertie has a terribly hard decision to make, as do I —"

"And so do I. I'm staying."

"No. Difficult as it is for me to say, the answer is no. There is no way you, or any of us, can stay."

"But Gram will be all alone." I started to shiver. "Don't you understand? She'll miss me."

"She'll miss you very much." He buttoned his jacket around me. "But she loves you enough to do what's best for you." Then he said very softly, "As do I.

"I promise you, Phoebe, as long as your grandmother is alive, somehow, some way, you'll get to see her.

"And I'll promise you something else. I'll make no definite decisions for myself until you're settled. You can trust me. You know that, don't you?"

I didn't answer, but sat shivering, even with Bishopp's jacket wrapped tightly around me.

I would never settle in, I knew that. I wanted to cry out, but I knew it would do no good. I was almost twelve and knew that I couldn't really take care of myself, and that whatever, "those that knew best" would prevail. For now. But from somewhere deep inside me I knew that one day I'd come home again. For good.

≈ ≈ ≈

Bishopp had decided we were to leave Lubelle County early in July, but things got held up for a number of reasons. Billy Hill hadn't registered the car properly, and when the clerk at the registry saw Billy's empty sleeve hanging down by his side, Mr. Hanks, the regional supervisor was called in.

"Well, now, Sergeant Hill," Mr. Hanks said to Billy, "I know there are some people in this town who give special privileges to you, seeing as you are Lubelle's local hero. But the Lubelle County Registry of AutoMObile Vee-hickles is not a people, it is an agency of the state, and as such, cannot treat you any different than any other person who walks through our doors."

Billy asked Mr. Hanks to accompany us to the car, where Billy asked me to help him put on "this goldarn contraption," as he called his prosthesis. He motioned me into the backseat of the car, invited Mr. Hanks to take the passenger's seat, and proceeded to demonstrate to Mr. Hanks how he could handle a car, prosthesis and all. But Mr. Hanks wouldn't budge.

"The law's the law," Mr. Hanks said. "You bring this vee-hickle back when you've got it working so as a one-armed man, and left-handed at that, can operate it within the confines of the law of Lubelle County, Georgia."

I started to say that Billy always drove it just the way it was, but Billy gave me a shove and told Mr. Hanks he'd be happy to do as he asked.

That took a while. Partly because there was only one mechanic in all of Lubelle County who could do the job. And then there was the house.

Bishopp had asked Miss Jean's nephew if he would be interested in advertising the house for rental until things were settled. "Why, sir," Miss Jean's nephew said, "I couldn't do that. No, sir, this house is in need of some loving care before my company could offer it." He told Bishopp he'd be happy to keep an eye on things for a few dollars a month. "But you be sure to close it up real good. Drain the water and such. Don't need no floods." Bishopp agreed. I was happy for that. I didn't want anybody else living in our house, even for a little while.

Getting the house ready to close up was a terrible job. Bertie kept saying that she and Bishopp weren't kids anymore and it took them longer to do the things they used to do, and that money was so tight, they couldn't afford to hire anybody to do the job.

Mornings were spent packing and cleaning. Bishopp had Billy pack some silver to be taken with us. Bertie washed and ironed every single piece of clothing and every single piece of linen she could find. She even washed and ironed Miss Jean's "personals" and had Billy and me take them on over to her.

"Remember, now," Bertie said as Billy and I got ready to go to Miss Jean's, "you be sure to tell her good-bye nicely. And tell her we're going to miss her. Especially —"

"I'm not telling her any such thing," I said, thinking Bertie was serious.

"You just hold on there," Bertie said. "I'm not

finished. I was about to say, especially her sweet, kind ways." Then she laughed and handed Billy a package.

And finally, there was Bishopp and Bertie's search for Gram's papers. Long after I was supposed to be asleep, I'd hear the two of them mumbling and rummaging around in Gram's room, or in the attic, or looking in closets that had been closed up for years.

One morning, as though I didn't know what was going on, I asked Bishopp what they were looking for. "Sneak," Miss Jean would have said. When he told me, I offered to help. That made me feel sneaky *and* guilty, especially when Bishopp asked me where I'd found my birth certificate. "In that old trunk," I said, pointing toward the trunk under the window.

"Anything else with it?" he asked, after he looked and found it empty. "Papers of any sort?"

"Nothing," I said and waited for that heavy feeling I always got in my chest when I lied. But the feeling didn't come.

"You're sure now, Phoebe?" Bishopp asked, his voice weary.

"I'm sure." I took a deep breath. Still I felt nothing.

Bishopp slammed the cover, thanked me for my help, then headed toward the stairs leading down from the attic. "Tell Bertie I'm off to see your grandmother," he called back. "I'll be back in time for supper."

I sat up in the attic for a long time wondering why

I didn't feel worse about lying. I'd never in my whole life lied to Bishopp. And then I understood. This wasn't a mean, hurtful lie, my not telling him about the papers and the letter with my father's address. It was a kind, helpful lie. A lie that would help all of us, because I knew deep down that nobody really wanted to find my father. Especially me.

PART TWO

July 1977:
The Journey Begins

Empty Gardens

7

*P*apers or not, the day came when Bishopp said it was time to go. It reminded me of the morning the moving men hauled Bosendorfer up to Gram's room, except there was no tea party. Everybody was in a terrible mood. Even Billy Hill. He kept ordering us around, telling us what positions to take in the car. Bertie would sit in the center seat, back, to balance the weight. I was to sit to her left. Suitcases to her right. Bishopp up front with him.

"Don't you be telling me where to sit, little brother," Bertie said, packing the last sandwich into the picnic hamper we were to take with us. "I'll sit where I darn well please."

Bishopp told Billy he'd be quite content to sit in the passenger's seat, but reminded Billy he was just the driver and not a platoon sergeant.

I wondered how Bishopp knew where we were going. When I asked him, all he'd say was, "To the far north." He'd put his arm around me and told me not to worry, that he was in charge of this journey.

This journey. A journey that was supposed to end when we found my father. A father I didn't know. A father who never wanted me. A father who wouldn't want me now. Or Bishopp.

At first I imagined that if we found my father, we'd all stay with him, because of what my father had said in one of the letters. That he was doing fine. That if my grandmother needed anything, she should just ask. But Bertie told me she would be leaving us in Okawala, Virginia, to live with her sister, Ginny Graham. Billy would go on with us, but once Bishopp and I had found my father, Billy would return to Okawala, too.

"How can you want to stay with her and not with me?" I'd asked Bertie.

"Mr. Graham's ailing and Ginny's been running the bakeshop. She needs help."

"What about your arthritis?"

Bertie laughed. "I sit down when I do my baking." Then she got real serious. "I need to get myself settled, sugar babe. And she needs more than my baking. She needs family around her."

"What about me? I'm your family, aren't I?"

"You sure are," she said, putting her arm around me. "Like my own." She looked down at me. "But you've got a daddy out there." She sighed a long sigh. "I wish things were different. But it's what I've got to do."

I tried feeling angry with Bertie, because when I'm angry about something I don't feel so sad and afraid. But it was hard to stay angry with her. She kept telling me she'd be sending for me, and that I could visit at Ginny's anytime. "Why, I'll send Billy on up to get you."

"And Bishopp, too."

A cloud would come over her face, but she'd say, "Bishopp, too."

The morning we were to leave, I stood in the foyer by the front door and looked around. The large mirror next to the parlor door was covered, and most of the paintings had been taken down. In their place great vacant shapes stood out against the grimy walls.

For the last several days, I'd gone into every room in the house, trying hard to lock into my mind a picture of each one. Especially my room and Gram's. Bosendorfer was still in Gram's room, covered up. The shades were drawn and the furniture draped with sheets. Bertie said it was so things wouldn't fade, but everything in our house was already faded and old. Seeing Gram's room like that reminded me of *Great Expectations,* one of the movies we'd seen at the Shady Lawn viewing room. Especially Miss Havisham's room. A shiver ran through me as I imagined dust covering everything, great cobwebs hanging from the ceiling, and mice crawling on and in Bosendorfer, nibbling away at the shawl until he was laid bare.

I went over to Gram's dresser and picked up her hairbrush. Some of Gram's hair was still tangled in it. I closed my eyes and brushed my hair, pretending Gram was behind me. "Sweet little bird of my heart," I said, my voice mimicking hers, "you'll not be gone long."

And then I answered, my voice quivering, my body trembling, "I love you, Gram. We'll be back. You'll see."

I put the brush in my pocket and ran from the room.

Everything in my room was covered, too. Bishopp told me I could take just about anything I wanted along. "That old Deusenberg has quite a large trunk," he'd said, knowing I'd need to take certain treasures with me. I did take some. Books and Gram's papers. But the rest I left waiting for me.

"Sugar babe," Bertie called from the bottom of the stairs, "we're ready."

I ran my hand over my bed and across my window seat, went in to say good-bye to old Bosendorfer, and walked down the back stairs into the kitchen. I looked around that room carefully, committing to memory the worn wooden floor, the old wooden cabinets with the shiny glass fronts. The blue-and-white-checked curtains Bertie had made. The big black stove that warmed the kitchen and Bishopp's pantry. I went into his pantry. He was closing the door to the top cabinet, the one he kept his apron in. "Shan't be needing this," he said softly. Then he smoothed his creamy-white linen jacket and hung it on its usual hanger behind the door. "Nor this."

"Maybe you should take it," I said.

"No. It belongs here."

He leaned against the pantry door, wearing what he called his old golf jacket. Everybody said Bishopp looked just like Ray Bolger, the farmhand who became the Scarecrow in *The Wizard of Oz*. And he did, especially in that jacket. It was too big for him and made his head look small. He looked around and for a minute I thought he was about to cry, but, of course, he didn't. He gathered himself up quickly and said, "Come. I have a few last-minute things to do."

He checked the doors and windows at least a dozen times. He checked the water pipes and stuffed steel wool in any open crevice he found. Billy Hill kept telling him it was a waste of time. "Them little mice will be running right through that stuff and right on in, come November."

Bishopp told Billy if he opened his mouth once more, he would stuff it with so much steel wool it would take a pack of elephants till next November to run on through to set his tongue loose.

Billy was quiet after that.

All of us were.

Bertie picked up the picnic hamper, took one last look at "her kitchen," and headed toward the door. I followed. The day was clear, the sun warm; the petunias in Bertie's window box swayed in the soft wind coming off the river. As we passed the back porch for the last time, I thought I heard Bertie sob, but when I looked over at her, I was wrong. She looked straight ahead, her fan in one hand, the picnic hamper in the other.

I turned and saw Bishopp locking the door. His shoulders were shaking. I started back.

"Phoebe," Bertie said, "you give that man his privacy." We walked slowly around the side of the house, toward the driveway where Billy Hill sat at the wheel of Gram's big old car.

"All set?" Billy called out.

We filed into the car, saying nothing, and took our places. Bertie next to the window behind Billy. Me at the back window behind Bishopp, the picnic hamper between us. Bishopp took his place in the passenger seat.

Billy started up the motor and guided the car down the driveway.

"Well," Billy Hill said, his voice soft and gentle, "I'm sure sorry to be leaving that old house. It was good to all of us."

Bertie started to cry. "Seems wrong somehow for us all to be going, leaving Olivia."

"Nothing is forever," Bishopp said, turning back, his eyes quickly darting to me, then back to Bertie. "Let's try to do what's best for all of us."

Something inside told me not to say I'd seen Bishopp cry, too. I reached out and took Bertie's hand. She looked over at me, tears running down her cheeks, and forced a smile. "I packed your favorite. Blackberry fool."

I squeezed her hand, then turned toward the window. The sun made the river glisten as though somebody had sprinkled tiny pieces of mirror into the water. I watched, my eyes squinting against the brightness, until Billy Hill turned onto the main road where the big oak leaves darkened everything.

Run for Your Life

8

Silence was our companion as we headed toward Route 106, the road that would take us to Gila Bend, where Billy could connect with Route 158, the route Bertie decided we would take. "If the good Lord came down and asked me to travel one of those super-highways, I'd say, 'Lord, only if you're driving,' " she'd said over and over again, whenever the journey was discussed. She was firm, even when Billy told her it would take us forever to get where we were going.

"We'll hit every small town from here to Okawala. I'm telling you, Sister, Route 495 is the way to go."

"And I am telling you that my behind will not sit itself in a car that's speeding along on some big high-way. Do I make myself understood, little brother?"

Bishopp kept out of that argument. He knew Bertie well enough to know once she'd made up her mind, there was little chance of changing it.

We bumped along and when we got to the road in Pine Park that led up to the Shady Lawn Rest Home, the stillness in the car made the sound of the car's motor seem like a train was riding alongside us.

We had said our good-byes to Gram the day before. It was sad because she was having one of her bad days. She hadn't recognized me, and as many times as Bishopp tried to explain about her slipping back into the past, I never got used to it. Especially that last day, knowing I'd probably not see her again for a long time. Maybe ever.

I leaned forward and put my arms around Bishopp, my head on his shoulder. He reached back and put his hand on my cheek. "I know, Phoebe, it's hard. Hardest for you. But remember what I promised you."

I tried doing that, but it didn't help. Especially since the day Billy and I went to Miss Jean. After we delivered her belongings, said our good-byes, and were in the car and ready to go, she came down the walk and poked her head in the window on Billy's side. She said something about Gram being all-out crazy to send me off with the hired help.

I'd wanted to leap from the car and punch her out, but Billy told me to keep my behind where it was, told Miss Jean to get hers moving, and headed the car on home.

"You're the crazy one!" I'd yelled back. "And you're the hired help, too!"

Billy had told me to cool down and that what Miss Jean thought didn't amount to a hill of beans.

But what if Gram had gone crazy? What if she forgot all about me? What if I never saw her again?

What if Bertie really did decide to stay with Ginny? Billy, too? What if my father didn't want me? But most of all, what if Bishopp and I couldn't stay together? The tears started again. It seemed that crying was all I did lately.

"Everything's going to be all right," Bishopp said.

"You'll stay with me, won't you?"

"As long as you need me."

"That will be forever," I said. "Right?"

He smiled a little smile and smoothed my hair the way he always did.

After a while, he handed me his handkerchief and suggested I get to work on the job he had assigned me for the duration of the trip. "It sometimes helps to keep busy, Phoebe. Why don't you give it a try."

I blew my nose and Bertie handed me the road atlas from my traveling case. Billy had reluctantly marked the way leading to Route 158. I was to be the navigator, keeping track of the roads Billy had marked and, when a turn was indicated, relaying the information to Bishopp, who along with Billy would be on the lookout.

It did help, but what helped even more was knowing Bishopp would be with me no matter what. Even knowing that, I was tempted not to tell him about the first turn I saw coming up. But even if Bishopp believed me, I knew it wouldn't take Billy long to figure out we were going wrong. He pretty much knew the way to Okawala.

"There's a right turn about five miles down the road," I said. Turned out we missed it anyway, because

Bishopp had busied himself, too, going over the budget he had worked out for the journey.

"Goldarn it," Billy said, turning the car back to the main road. "All this would be unnecessary if Sister back there would be a bit more reasonable."

"Watch your language," Bertie said. "And Sister back here is as reasonable as she's going to get."

Bishopp then proceeded to tell Billy and Bertie that he was not about to listen to their carping all the way to Okawala. "We do not have the luxury of traveling by rail, where one can change one's seat or step into the dining car when one is irked beyond one's tolerance."

Bertie hated it when Bishopp got into his one-knows-that-one-cannot-do-what-one-wants-to-do-when-one-wants-to-do-it moods.

She nudged me and rolled her eyes and the two of us laughed until Bishopp told us to be still, that he had some serious business he wanted to get into. He had worked hard on the strict budget we were to follow. There would be so much allotted for each night's lodging. So much for each day's food. So much for gas and oil for the car. So much for incidentals.

He looked up from his budget book and said, "What with Bertie's preserves and such, food money should go quite far."

He did see a problem looming quite soon if we didn't agree on the matter of lodging. "We cannot afford to rent two rooms each night. We simply don't have enough money."

He then went on to say he realized sharing a single room would be an inconvenience for all of us, but felt if we all maintained a reasonable amount of good humor, it could be done quite nicely.

"Are we all in agreement?"

We all said yes. Bertie did have one reservation, which she said could be taken care of by nightfall. "Billy, next five-and-dime store you pass, see that you make a stop."

When Billy was back on the right road, he turned on the radio and we listened to Joe Cudjoe's weather report, the local news, and Joe Cudjoe singing along with every song he played, making up his own words as he went along. Bishopp never had appreciated Joe Cudjoe's sense of humor, and after a while Bishopp, his voice on edge, said, "How long must we be subjected to this?"

"Amen to that," Bertie said.

Billy didn't seem to pay any attention. "I went to school with him," he said. "Skinny little runt of a guy. Always whining to the teachers about how the rest of us teased him about his peculiar voice. Kind of high. Like a girl's almost. Got even higher when the rest of us were struggling to keep ours from hitting bottom."

"His hasn't changed much," Bishopp said.

"You remember him, Sister?"

"I was long gone by that time. Those days I thought I'd seen the last of Georgia." She shook her head slowly. "From the time I met Olivia, my life took more twists and turns than the Mississippi River." She turned to me. "But we sure had us some good times."

I knew that. Bertie and Gram had told me how they'd met in New York City. They were standing in line waiting to be called to audition for an operetta. From the start, they liked one another and through the years kept in touch. When Bertie decided she'd had enough, that her singing days were over, Gram asked if she'd be interested in traveling with her, taking charge of her affairs. When my mother came along, Bertie took charge there, too. "We had fun in those days," Gram would say. Then Gram would get all solemn-like and say, "You know, Bertie should have sung at the Met. Her voice was as good as mine." When I'd ask Gram why she hadn't, she'd shake her head and say, "Because people are fools."

"I have had all I can take," Bishopp said, when Joe Cudjoe began to wail, "How much is that doggie in the window, the one with the wiggly, waggly tail? . . ." He leaned over and flipped the radio off.

"It sure is a mystery to me how Joe Cudjoe ever got to where he is," Billy said. "Never had a personality that I could detect." He shrugged. "Hey, maybe he's changed. People do."

"They sure do," Bertie said, looking over at me. "Why, every time I look at you, you look like you've sprung up another inch." She poked me in the ribs. "But no fat anywhere."

"Was my father skinny?"

"As I recall, he was." She smiled. "You getting hungry?"

I shook my head. The truth was I was feeling kind of sick to my stomach. This was the longest ride I'd taken in a while, and my stomach was jumping around.

"You looking for the next turn?" Billy called back to me.

"It's not for a while. Not till we get near Cairo."

"Cairo?" Bishopp said, laughing. "I didn't know we were going to Egypt."

Bishopp almost never said anything funny. It sounded so queer to hear him telling a joke, well, almost a joke, that I laughed along with Billy and Bertie, even though my stomach felt terrible.

I tried not to think about it as we whizzed by great fields with nothing but rows and rows of corn. We passed farms where horses grazed in the fields. But when we came to a railroad crossing and Billy slammed his foot on the brake, my breakfast suddenly left me and went all over the car.

Bishopp told Billy to pull over to the side of the road. Bertie got out of the car and came around to my side, and she and Bishopp helped me out of the car.

"There, there, now," Bishopp said gently, "it's all right. We'll get you something that will take care of this as soon as we get to the next town."

Billy got out of the car, gagging all the while, and opened the trunk so Bertie could get me fresh clothes. She held a blanket around me as I changed. Bishopp kept telling me I'd be just fine, and that I must rest for a while by the side of the road until I felt better. "I used to get motion sickness when I was your age," he said.

"But back then, I was traveling in a wagon." He put his hand under my chin, lifted my face, and gently pressed a cool cloth to my forehead. "I suppose you believe that, Phoebe, seeing as you think I'm an old relic."

I gave him a half laugh, despite feeling just awful.

When I'd finished changing into fresh clothes and the car was wiped clean, Bertie took the picnic hamper from the backseat, spread out the blanket, and we sat down.

"Drink a little," Bertie said, pouring some tea from a thermos. "It'll help."

I sipped a little, and Bertie asked me if the sight of food would make me sicker. I shook my head, so the rest of them ate some fruit.

Bishopp told me to lay my head in his lap to see if I could fall asleep for just a bit. "That will settle you."

I closed my eyes and was just about to doze off, when Billy yelled. "Jeeeeeeeee-sus! It's coming right at us."

He pulled me up from Bishopp's lap. "Forget the food!" he yelled. "Get in the car before he mows us down!"

We raced back to the car, Bertie and Bishopp at our heels.

When we were safely in the car, windows rolled up, still trying to get our breath, I looked out and saw what we had been running from.

The biggest cow I'd ever seen. She stomped onto

the blanket and over to the car, banged her snout against Bishopp's window, bared her teeth, and stared in at us. We sat motionless. After a while, she turned, flicking flies away from the hump on her shoulder with her tail. She stuck her snout inside the picnic hamper, then poked around until everything in the hamper spilled onto the blanket.

"That's a Brahman, sure as anything," Billy said. "You don't fool with one of them bulls."

"Bull?" I said. "I thought it was a cow."

"No sirree," Billy said. "That sure is no cow."

"How can you tell?"

"Well," Billy said, looking over at Bishopp, "I, I . . ."

Without a warning, the bull turned, bent his head low, and rammed the side of the car with his horns.

"Dear Jesus," Bertie said, making the sign of the cross, "deliver us. Please."

"Start the motor," Bishopp said.

The bull backed away and went back to the hamper.

"There goes all that good food," Bertie said, sighing, as he crushed a jar of Bertie's preserves beneath his hooves. "Why, there must be at least ten good dollars going to waste out there."

We sat there until the bull got tired, pushed against the car window one last time, then slowly ambled back to where it had come from.

Bertie was right. There wasn't one single piece of

food he hadn't gotten into or stamped on. Billy gathered up the blanket and the picnic hamper, put all the spoiled food into a bag, and we started up again.

Bishopp instructed Billy to stop every once in a while, at which times I'd get out of the car, walk around a bit, take some deep breaths, and then we'd be on our way.

By the time we got to a town, everybody was starving, including me. Bishopp got me some pills that were guaranteed to prevent motion sickness, then he decided to treat us all to some McDonald's hamburgers.

After we finished up at McDonald's, Bertie searched out a Woolworth's, told us to wait in the car, and when she came out, she waved a clothesline back and forth. "Well," she said, after settling herself in her chosen place behind Billy, "Our lodging problem is solved. You can drive on, little brother."

With a Little Help from My Friends

9

We drove until dark, my stomach cooperating all the while with the help of the pills Bishopp had purchased. Bishopp had decided we were to spend the first night in a small town called Bloomstown. He found the name of an inexpensive motel in the travel guide he had purchased before we left home.

"The Whistling Swan Motel," he read as we headed toward Bloomstown, "is a small but comfortable family-owned motel on the outskirts of Bloomstown. Have your choice of single or double room in motel, or one-room efficiency-type cabin equipped with one or two double beds, depending on your needs. Quaint, quiet, and comfortable. Restaurant on premises. Modest rates — $12.50 per night per double, each additional person only $1.00. Reservations not necessary."

"Sounds good to me," Billy said. "Where do we turn off?"

We didn't have to turn off. The Whistling Swan was on the main road. As Billy pulled under a sign that said, "THE WH STLING SWA   MOT L," trucks roared past us and headed toward the rear of the parking lot, where the restaurant was situated. Billy flashed the highbeams on the restaurant sign that read, "TRUCK STOP — GOOD FOOD — SERVED 24 HOURS."

"I thought you said this was a quiet place, Bish," Billy said.

"I was merely repeating what was reported in the travel guide."

"Well, I can see now why reservations aren't too much of a problem," Bertie said, heaving herself out of the car.

Bishopp said we all should stretch our legs and go into the office with him. When we walked in, the man standing behind the counter, who identified himself as the owner, put his hand over his mouth and in a loud whisper said to a woman sitting in the rear of the office, "Get a look at this crew." Then he turned to us and asked Bishopp what he could do for us. He told Bishopp the guide we had was at least five years old and the rates had gone up. "Cost you $15.00 a night and $2.50 for extra towels, seein' as there's four of you."

"This guide is most certainly not five years old," Bishopp said, putting the cover under the man's nose. Then he flipped through some pages and pointed to the ad he had seen. "Furthermore, the price you quote is not what you state in your ad."

"Look, mister, I don't care what the ad says. Take

it or leave it. You folks stayin' here ain't gonna make or break me."

Bishopp looked from Bertie to Billy to me. He shrugged, turned back to the owner, and said, "We'll take it."

"Ep," the owner called out to a lady sitting behind the counter, "get two towels and two facecloths out of the back room. These dandies'll be stayin' at Cabin Number Four." Then he turned back to Bishopp. "Checkout time is nine o'clock sharp, else you get charged for a extra day." He held out his hand. "I get paid in advance. Cash."

We tried to keep our humor up, but it was hard. The cabin was damp and dingy, the carpet so worn and wavy that Billy tripped and went sprawling. His prosthesis hit the floor first. "The Lord's with us," Billy said as Bishopp knelt to help him up. "Could've been my head." He grinned up at Bishopp. "We'll sue for the extra $2.50."

When Billy got settled, I looked around the cabin. There were two chairs covered with orange and gold material that was dirty and worn, and a table covered with a shabby plastic tablecloth. Bertie cleaned up the cooking area as best she could and then asked Billy to get some of the food she had packed in the trunk. Bishopp and I made up the extra bed, and when we had all gotten washed up, we sat down at the table.

Bertie had filled biscuits with ham and her special relish. She opened a jar of peaches and made hot tea.

When everything was set, Bertie reached out and took my hand. I was puzzled. Bertie always said a prayer before we ate, but we never held hands. She motioned for me to take Bishopp's hand. Then she reached out for Billy's; he took Bishopp's, and when we were all joined together, Bertie bowed her head and said, "Bless us, dear Jesus, as we travel on this journey. Be our companion. Give us strength and guidance along the way." I looked around the room at the two lumpy beds covered with thin, muddy spreads, at the walls covered with knotty pine. I closed my eyes and pretended we were sitting in Bertie's kitchen back home.

"One more thing, Lord," Bertie went on. "Deliver us from places like this. For that we will be eternally grateful."

She laughed and squeezed my hand. I squeezed Bishopp's; he squeezed Billy's; Billy squeezed Bertie's.

"Amen!" she said. "Let's eat."

And we *were* home.

Bad Side of the Moon

10

When we'd finished our meal, we helped Bertie clean up and then we got ready for bed. At Bertie's insistence, I was the first to use the bathroom. I ran the hot water, but in about two minutes it ran cold. I stood in the tub, the lukewarm water barely covering my toes, washed myself quickly, and got into my nightgown.

Billy was next, then Bishopp, and last Bertie. When she'd finished, she rummaged around in her pocketbook and came up with the bag from Woolworth's. She had purchased two large suction hooks that she proceeded to put on opposite walls. Then she fastened the clothesline to the hooks, took the spreads from the beds, and hung them over the line.

"There," she said. "At least we'll have a measure of privacy." Then she knelt down at the side of our bed, closed her eyes, and lowered her head. I always said my prayers in bed, but that night I knelt beside Bertie. She reached out and put her hand over mine, her eyes still closed, her head still lowered.

I had so much I wanted God to do for me. He already knew that Bishopp and I were to stay together. But then there were Bertie and Billy. I knew Bertie really felt she had to go to live with Ginny Graham. Billy, too. But He could help me change their minds, because what I really wanted God to do was to get us all back home with Gram.

I finished bargaining with God and got into bed. Bertie still knelt praying. Lights from passing traffic shone through the flimsy curtains, and just as Bertie got into bed beside me, a truck roared past the cabin, followed by a loud crash.

"Good Lord!" Bertie said, pushing herself out of bed. "What was that?"

Billy was outside before Bishopp was out of bed, and the three of us ran to the door. A truck had hit a tree and we could hear somebody yelling and cursing. It was the owner of the Whistling Swan.

"How many times have I told that horse's ass of a son of yours not to park in this here lot? I'm tellin' you, Ep, he does that one more time —" The moon was full, and in its light the owner saw Billy standing beside our car. "You got some business out here, nigger?"

Without a word, Bertie flew out the door, the night breeze wrapping her nightgown around her legs. "Billy," she shouted. "Pay no mind."

Billy did pay no mind. To Bertie. He ran over to the owner, picked him up by his belt, and held him at arm's length.

"You were saying, sir?" Billy said, his voice loud

enough to be heard over the roar of any truck. "I thought I heard something ugly, and I've been known to toss a man a country mile when I hear something as ugly as that."

"Billy," Bertie shouted. "Put him down. Now."

"You take yourself inside, Sister. This may take a while."

But it didn't. I couldn't hear the man's apology, but I did hear Billy say, "Apology accepted." Then he kind of twirled the man around once or twice and gently placed him back on the ground.

Billy headed back to the cabin, Bertie following. "Good night," he called back to the owner. "You sleep tight now."

Bertie pushed Billy through the door. Her face was as angry as I'd ever seen it. "You gone crazy?" she said. "You know what kind of country we're in here and you go out and do a dumb thing like that."

"Calm down, Sister. Nobody talks to me like that."

"You think that fool is worth your anger?"

Billy started to say something, but Bertie went over to him and as big as he was, pushed him into one of the chairs. "You listen to me, little brother. You got more than yourself to think of. You got this child. You hear me? You got me. And you got Bishopp. So when you feel like playing hero you best think long and hard. You hearing me?"

Billy didn't answer.

"I'm telling you, I'd as soon Bishopp drive that

car, bad as he is, and send you on your way than worry myself sick that you might do something that could bring harm to this child."

Billy was quiet for a while, then he reached out and pulled Bertie onto his lap, kissed her, said she was right, and that from here on in, he'd watch his p's and q's.

She tried to stay angry, but when Billy started to bounce her around on his knees, and Bishopp and I started to laugh, she broke down. "Ninny," she said, laughing out loud. "I told you some of your brains departed along with your arm." She gave him a quick kiss, then reached out to Bishopp and me and asked us to give her the old heave-ho.

"Well, now," Bishopp said, after Bertie was back on her feet, "I think we've had enough excitement for one evening. I suggest we all get some sleep."

But sleep was impossible for me. I kept thinking about what happened. "Stupid old man," I muttered. "Why would he say something like that?"

"You say something?" Billy whispered.

"I said he was a stupid old man to call you a nigger."

"Hey, Phoeb, there have been lots of stupid old men. But Bertie's right. Fighting won't change a thing."

I thought about that for a while, and about the fighting Billy had done in the war for people he didn't even know. Even people like that stupid old man. It made me angrier.

"You go to sleep now," Billy said. "We got a ways to go tomorrow."

I shut my eyes and tried, but sleep still wouldn't come. Trucks kept rumbling by, shaking the cabin. The beds creaked. Strange sounds came from under the cabin. I sat up in bed and whispered over to Billy. He whispered back that they were probably opossums or some such animal. Then he got up and looked out the window.

"What are you doing?"

"Shhhh. I thought I heard somebody out by the car."

"Did you lock it?"

"Heck, Phoeb, locks don't prevent much of anything," he said in a loud whisper. "And what'd I tell you about getting some sleep?"

"You're the one who needs sleep," I whispered back. "You drove all day."

"Don't worry about me. Since the war, I only sleep three, four hours at most." He sighed a deep sigh.

After a few minutes, I whispered, "Billy, I'm sorry your arm got blown away."

"So am I, Phoeb. But like I always say, I'm still here." He laughed softly. "And the one that stayed put does one heck of a job."

I thought of the owner of the Whistling Swan, his feet dangling as Billy held him, and I laughed so hard I had to bury my face in the pillow so as not to wake Bertie and Bishopp.

When I finally stopped, I said good night to Billy and he to me. I snuggled up to Bertie and waited for sleep to come. The cabin was still, except when a truck roared by, and I was just about to close my eyes when Billy pushed the spreads apart, crept over to the door, opened it, and peered outside. I slid out of bed and went over to him. "What's the matter?"

"Nothing yet. But I got my suspicions, so I'm not taking my eyes off that car." He pulled a chair over in front of the window. "You get back in bed. Go on now."

I didn't move. Something had been on my mind for a time.

"Billy," I whispered, "how did you know that was a bull and not a cow?"

He didn't answer.

"Billy?" I whispered. "Did you hear me?"

I walked around to the front of the chair and waited until the lights from one of the trucks lit up the room.

Billy's eyes were closed.

"You sleeping, Billy?"

I knew he wasn't, because something like that always happened when I asked a question like that of anybody. They pretended to fall either deaf, mute, or asleep. Billy did all three.

On the Road Again

11

*W*e made sure we were out of the Whistling Swan well before nine o'clock. Billy told us he'd stayed up most of the night, and it was a good thing he had. Ep's son came sneaking around the car about four o'clock, crowbar in hand, set to break into the trunk.

"All I had to do was shine that big old flashlight in his face and ask him if he'd like me to give him the ride I offered his daddy earlier in the evening. Then I turned the flashlight off and told him if he was still there when I turned it on, I'd be happy to oblige."

Bishopp decided that we'd eat on the road rather than risk an altercation at the motel's restaurant. As soon as we got settled in the car, he took out his budget book and began figuring. "Bertie," he said, after a while, "how much food did we lose to the bull?"

"Mmmnnnn. Last night's supper and this morning's breakfast. Four or five jars of preserves. Some blackberry fool." She looked over at me. "Sorry, sugar babe . . . and some odds and ends."

"The tea and the thermos," I added.

"Good Lord," Bertie said, "what a waste."

"Well, what's gone is gone," Bishopp said. "We'll just have to watch every penny from today on." He turned and looked at me. "Did you take your motion sickness pill?"

I nodded.

"Are you hungry?"

"I'm starving."

I'd just about gotten the words out of my mouth when I saw a sign that read: "SPECIAL — Two eggs, grits, toast, juice & coffee/tea/or milk — 69 cents. Get your fill at Phil's Grill — straight ahead — only four miles down the road."

"What do you think, Bertie?" Bishopp asked.

I turned to Bertie, put my hands together as though in prayer, and whispered, "Please."

She laughed and said, "That's just fine."

"One thing's for sure," I said, "if we get to my father's, we won't have to do all this worrying about money."

Bishopp turned and looked at Bertie, then over at me. "What on earth do you mean?"

"He's got money. Lots of it."

"And how would you know that?"

I almost said "from the letter," but stopped myself. I shrugged. "I don't know for sure. I'm just hoping."

The heavy feeling settled in my chest this time.

"Phoebe," he said, his voice gentle, "what difference would it make?"

Lots, I wanted to say. Like you being able to stay

if we ever find him. You could be his butler. And he could get Bertie to some big doctor who would take care of her arthritis. Billy could have a whole garage full of cars to drive and take care of. Gram could come to live with us. Or my father could fix up our house so we all could live back there. But all I did was shrug and say, "No difference."

Then I thought about the letters. My father said he had loved my mother so much he could never love anybody else as much again. As always, when I got to thinking about him, my stomach felt sick, and even though it was empty and growling, my appetite had disappeared.

"Here she be," Billy said, pulling into the parking lot of Phil's Grill. "I'm so hungry I could eat a horse."

"Maybe you will," Bertie said. "I never trust what restaurants put in their food." She looked over at me. "Help me out, will you, sweetie? It's getting harder and harder to haul myself out of this old machine."

Billy hopped out of the car, and before Bishopp could get the door opened for me, Billy had helped Bertie out and we headed for the restaurant.

Under a Blanket of Blue

12

*W*hen we got into Phil's, the smell of bacon frying and coffee brewing brought back my appetite.

Bishopp led us to a big booth at the back of the restaurant. I slid in next to Bertie. Billy tapped his hand in time to the music playing from one of the jukeboxes. He leaned over to me and sang, "Stomp your feet, move real fast, do the two-step mamou —"

"Shush," Bertie said, handing the menu to Bishopp. "There's nothing cheap on this menu besides the paper it's printed on."

Bishopp glanced at the menu, then up at the signs hanging on the walls. "Doesn't seem to be posted either, but they must honor their own ad."

"Like the Whistling Swan?" Bertie said. "Nothing but a big fat lie that one was."

As soon as the waitress came to take our order, Bishopp said we'd take four specials, two with coffee, one with tea, and one with milk.

"What specials you talkin' about?"

"The sixty-nine-cent specials," I said. "The one I saw advertised on the road sign."

"Oh, that," she said, fluffing out her already fluffy hair. "That's only on special between midnight and three in the A.M. That's for our truck trade." She pulled her pencil from behind her ear. "What'll it be?"

"Give us a moment or two, please," Bishopp said.

"I am out of here in five minutes," she said, putting her pencil back on her ear, "so you all make it fast."

We *did* make it fast. Out the door. Billy drove until we spotted a Piggly Wiggly supermarket, where we bought enough food to feed us both breakfast and noon dinner, and a new thermos filled with tea, for less than eight dollars. We drove until we saw a sign that said, "Rest Area —Rest Rooms — Telephones." Billy pulled in and parked the car, and just before we got out, Bishopp said we should stay put while he did a quick check of the area to make sure there were no bulls in sight. Bishopp got out of the car, put his hand up on his forehead as though he were searching, took exaggerated steps in all directions, then announced that it was safe for the rest of us to get out of the car. "Watch where you step," he warned. "Wet patches here and there."

"You're getting to be quite a comedian," Bertie said, laughing and handing him the bags of food from Piggly Wiggly. "Livia would've gotten a kick out of you stalking bulls."

Bertie was right about Gram getting a kick out of Bishopp. He never acted like that. It was funny, but in a way it was also too strange to me.

"Follow me," Bishopp said, leading the way toward the picnic tables that were scattered all over the grass. When Bertie found one she felt was clean enough to eat from, she spread out our food, said a little prayer, and we ate our breakfast.

As soon as Bishopp finished his second cup of tea, he took his budget book from his pocket and, shaking his head, a frown covering his face, turned the pages. "Prices certainly vary from place to place," he said. "At the pace we're spending, if we don't keep to our time schedule, we might well run out of funds."

"Please, God —"

Bishopp looked over at me. "We'll manage, Phoebe," he said, misreading my prayer. "It's not for you to worry about."

I kind of nodded at him and said I'd try not to.

Bishopp poured himself the last of the tea from the thermos, put his budget book into his pocket, and reached for the road map. "Perhaps there's a better road to travel up north than the one we're on." He glanced over at Bertie. "I know. No highways."

"Hey, Phoeb," Billy said, swinging his leg over the bench. "How about you and me going down to that there pond?" He pointed to a small pond that had a sign, "Two-Catch Limit," posted. "We'll catch us a couple of fish for supper. I am tired of all this store-bought food."

Bertie smiled over at me. "Why don't you get those fishing lines you put in the trunk? Do you good to have a little fun."

The morning was bright, the sun warm on our

backs, and the pool was so clear, we could see the fish swimming around. But no matter what we did, we just couldn't catch one. Finally, I took off my sneakers and socks, rolled up my pants, and waded in. Billy followed. We stood still, so as not to disturb the fish, waited for several minutes, bent down slowly, held our hands just above the water, and tried to catch one in our hands. We did it about a hundred times, but every time we grabbed one, the fish would slip out of our hands and back into the pond. "Next time, Phoeb, is the time we're going to do it," Billy kept saying. We were just about to give up when Bishopp came to the edge of the pond. "Time to leave," he called. "I think I've found a road that will shorten our trip considerably."

"That's what I didn't want, God," I whispered, wading back to shore, thinking how great it would be if I could close my eyes and open them to find myself back home, the river at my back, our house straight ahead. Gram up in her room playing Bosendorfer, Bertie in her kitchen, Bishopp in his pantry. Billy tinkering with the car.

"Come along, Phoebe," Bishopp said. "We're wasting precious time."

After everything was loaded back into the car, Bishopp pointed out the new route to Billy. Billy looked at it for a long while, not thoroughly convinced that Bishopp was right.

"Does appear to be a bit shorter," Billy said, "but seems to me we'll be going through every small town in every state we drive through." He turned to Bertie and tried to convince her once again that highway travel was safe, that it would cut our travel time by days. She remained adamant. "No highways," she said, and for that I was grateful.

Billy started the car, but when he put his foot on the gas nothing happened, except the sound of the tires spinning.

"What the —" Billy said, giving the car more gas.

Still nothing.

"Well, I'll be," he said, getting out of the car. He checked all the wheels, came around to Bishopp's side of the car, and said, "We're stuck."

Bishopp got out and walked to the rear of the car. I could hear Billy say something about the mud in Georgia having the reputation of fattening the pockets of every tow-truck operator in the state.

Bishopp kept shaking his head back and forth, the frown on his face deeper than ever. "We can get it out without a tow truck," he said.

Bertie and I got out of the car. Billy got back in. Bishopp told me to tell Billy to start up the car again and give it the gas. He did. Bishopp pushed. The wheels spun. Bertie and I joined Bishopp behind the car. Billy gave it the gas. We pushed. The wheels spun again. Billy switched places with Bishopp. The wheels whined.

I sat behind the wheel, Billy giving me instructions as to what I should do. I did. Still the wheels spun. All three of them pushed again and again, but the wheels remained in place.

Bishopp slumped against the car in defeat. Bertie went over to the nearest bench and sat down, wiping her forehead with the hem of her dress. Sitting at the wheel of Gram's old car made me think of the times I would sit on top of Bosendorfer, Bertie and Bishopp pushing him to where he wanted to be, Gram asking Bosendorfer if he was happy in his new place. All of us sitting down to have tea and sandwiches. I felt so homesick, I wanted to cry.

We waited for a long while before trying to get the wheels to cooperate. Bishopp hoped the sun would dry up enough of the mud to get us moving, leaving the problem behind us. But that didn't happen. We were still waiting at noon, but even then, with the air dry as cotton balls and the sun as hot as it was going to get, the mud held the tires fast. Weary, we sat down and ate our dinner, and after we'd eaten our fill, Bishopp reluctantly called a towing service.

"Lucky we stopped at a rest area with a telephone," Billy said when Bishopp came back to where we were sitting.

Bishopp didn't say anything, but the frown on his face did.

We sat quietly until the tow truck arrived, and within minutes the wheels were freed. Billy was right about the mud in Georgia.

"That'll be thirty-five eighty-two," the tow-truck operator said, smiling so widely I could see his back teeth. "The eighty-two cents bein' tax."

Even though Bishopp frowned and I knew how

worried he was, I was glad. Maybe now we'd have to go back.

Bishopp counted out the proper amount, handed the operator the money, and asked for a receipt. "Don't carry 'em around with me," he said, stuffing the money into his rear pocket. "Now you all have yourselves a good day, you hear."

It was definitely not a good day, nor a good night. We bounced along the road Bishopp had decided we should take, trying to make up the time we had lost. We ate our supper in the car, and when I looked in the guidebook for a motel, there wasn't one anywhere near the road we had taken. We ended up sleeping in the car, but not before Billy made sure there was solid ground beneath us.

Long after everybody had fallen asleep, I looked up at the sky through the rear window. There was a full moon and lots of stars. It made me think of all the times Bishopp and I had looked through Bishopp's telescope back home. It seemed so strange to be looking at the moon from Gram's car in a place that had no name, when that same moon was shining over our house in Lubelle County. The same moon that was shining somewhere off the coast of Maine where my father lived. I wanted to feel there was something mystical about it, something joining us all together, but all I felt was the loneliness I'd felt earlier. I wrapped the car blanket around me, snuggled up against Bertie's warm body, and counted the sounds of the night until I slept.

You've Been a Good Old Wagon, but You've Done Broke Down

13

The next morning we got off to an early start, stopping to use the restrooms at the nearest roadside rest area. Bertie made a big fuss about there not being enough toilet tissue to cover the seats. She went back to the car and brought back paper napkins and got to work.

When everybody had washed up and we were settled, Bertie got out her blackberry preserves and spread it on the last of her biscuits, but they were so stale I couldn't bite into mine, so I licked the jam from it. Billy did the same, telling Bertie that when she got settled in Okawala she could make herself quite a pretty penny selling the preserves at Ginny's bakeshop. Bertie hushed him quickly, but not before my stomach got that hot feeling, the feeling it always had when I thought about Bertie leaving. Bishopp must have sensed that because he did something he never did before, at least that I ever saw him do. He licked the jam from the biscuit, then scooped out a huge spoonful from the jar Bertie was holding, put the spoon into his mouth, and in one large gulp, the jam disappeared. I laughed so hard, the orange juice I was drinking came spilling out of my mouth and my nose all over my clothes.

Bertie scolded Bishopp and told him since he was responsible for the mess I had created, he'd have to clean up, but she laughed as she said it. As soon as everything was cleared up and I had changed my clothes, we were on the road again. We hadn't gone a mile when the car started to give Billy trouble. Billy blamed it on the mud. Bishopp blamed it on the tow-truck operator. But whatever it was, the car kept stalling, and every time it did, Bertie would say we never should have left Lubelle County in a car old enough to be drawing a pension.

Billy told her to calm down, that at the next available gas station he'd pull in to have the whole car checked out. Every time Billy stopped at a light, the car would stall and people would toot and holler out at Billy to trade the car in for a horse. He'd yell back and then Bertie would tell him to hold his tongue. Billy would remind her that he was driving the car, and in that capacity he was in charge. She would remind Billy that she was his big sister, and in that capacity she could tell him what was what. Bishopp, generally tolerant of these little feuds, and usually stopping them by going into his one-cannot-do-as-one-wishes routine, told Billy and Bertie to shut up. Bertie, of course, was not about to, reminding Bishopp that she was not, nor had she ever been, under his authority. "I was with Olivia long before you came into the picture." Bishopp wearily acknowledged that fact and apologized.

Back home, Bishopp could handle anything, but here, driving in Gram's car on a lonely road far from Lubelle County, he worried constantly about our not having enough money. He seemed almost as scared about not getting to my father as I was about getting to him. I felt sorry for Bishopp, but I knew that running out of money was the only way we'd turn back and go home.

When Billy spotted a sign that said, "Rita's Restaurant — Truck Stop," he asked us all to pray that there was a gas station on the premises, and no red lights between us and Rita's. Billy had forgotten to include railroad crossings, because we got stuck at one.

It took forever for the train to go through, and when a boxcar went by with a sign, "MOTHER KELLY'S HOME-MADE JAMS AND JELLIES," Billy said there was a way to put money troubles behind us.

"Remember that movie we saw at Shady Lawn?" he said. "The one about the salesman who took this little girl traveling with him to help him sell Bibles?"

Bishopp didn't remember, but Bertie and I did.

He turned to Bertie. "How many jars of preserves do you have?"

"Two dozen. Maybe more. Why?"

"Because we can sell them, just the way the girl sold Bibles."

"That is absurd," Bishopp said.

"Hold on, now," Billy said. "Hear me out.

"This Moses guy taught her exactly how to get a sale every time. 'Ma'am,' the girl would say when somebody kept the screen door locked against them, 'is Mr. Hackett at home?' "

Bertie reached for the leather strap behind the driver's seat and hauled herself forward. "If I remember correctly, he was a liar and a thief —"

"Let me finish, Sister.

"Miz Hackett would say that Mr. Hackett had passed on. Then the girl would look up and raise her hands to heaven and say, 'Lord, be praised. I'm here where I should be. I'm at 287-A Hickory Place with Miz Elvira Hackett, just like Mr. Hackett wanted.' Then she'd tell Miz Hackett that her husband had ordered a deluxe Bible, just for her.

"Why, folks like Miz Hackett almost pushed their hands through the screen trying to get the little girl and the Bible in the door —"

"You think I'm going to be the little girl?" I said, leaning over toward Billy. "You think I'm going to sell Bertie's preserves? Not me."

"Not I," said Bishopp. "And of course you're not. Nobody is."

"I could if I wanted to," I said. "Remember how I sold all those packages of seeds back home?"

"To your grandma and Bishopp and Billy and me," Bertie said.

"I'll bet I would have sold them even if you hadn't bought —"

"Nobody is selling anything," Bishopp said. "Is that clear?"

"Well, I still think it's a good idea," Billy said. "Better than praying over every penny we spend."

Bishopp held up his hands. "I repeat. There will be no door-to-door sales. Not preserves. Not Bibles. We'll manage."

Billy said something about the Lord being more humble about people trying to help themselves than some people he knew.

Bertie patted Billy's back. "Your heart's in the right place, little brother."

I sat back and relaxed.

When we finally spotted Rita's Restaurant, the car barely made it into the parking lot. Billy pulled into the first empty spot and we got out to stretch our legs.

"Food must be good if truckers stop here," Billy said.

"That's an old wives' tale," Bertie said, as I helped her out of the car. "There were more trucks than this at the Whistling Swan, and I'll bet their food was awful."

"Never got the chance to taste it," Billy said, taking off his prosthesis and rubbing his stump. "Dang thing gets so sore at times, and today is one of those times."

"This must have been a pretty place in its day," Bertie said, looking around.

I thought it still was, even though, according to Bertie, it needed lots of tender loving care. It reminded me of the houses I'd seen when Gram had taken me to Memphis. Lots of gingerbread detailing all over and a porch that went right across the front of the house. The door and the shutters were painted green, and even though the paint was chipped the color that was left was as green as the weeping willows down by the river back home. But it was the upstairs that seemed to me to be best of all. High up near the roof was a small window, rounded at the top. A lace curtain was blowing from the opening, and above that hung what looked like a birdcage.

"Hey," somebody called from inside, "will the two applicants get their behinds on in here? I ain't got all day."

"Who said that?" Bishopp asked.

"Darned if I know," Billy said.

The door swung open and a man stood in the doorway, a cigarette dangling from his lips, a big chef's hat on his head. "What're they doing to me down there? I told them I only needed two people." He took off his hat and scratched his head. "Look, I told you I ain't got all day," he said, the cigarette bobbing up and down. "Which two are applying for the jobs?"

Billy started toward the door, but Bishopp said to stay where he was.

"Okay," the man said, smoothing the few strands of hair he had across the top of his head, "which one of you is the cook?"

Bishopp walked toward him. We followed.

"Well, you don't look like no cook." He tossed the cigarette on the ground, putting it out with his shoe. "But I'm willing to give you a try."

"I'm afraid there's been a bit of a misunderstanding," Bishopp said. "We're looking for a gas station."

"You mean to tell me you're not from the unemployment office?"

Bishopp told him we were from Lubelle County, traveling north, that our car was giving us trouble, that we needed a gas station with a repairman on the premises, and that we could do with some breakfast.

He shook his head back and forth. "Can't help you. Don't have a gas pump. Don't have a repairman. Don't have a cook."

He told Bishopp that there was a gas station about two miles down the road, but their repairman was not known for his reliability. "Only comes in when he has the urge to —"

"Mack!" a woman shouted from inside Rita's. "The stove's on fire."

"Jeeeruselum," he said, planting his hat back on his head and running back in the door. "There go the eggs."

We stood motionless as their voices blasted out of the open windows. "You're gonna burn this place down if you don't get somebody who knows how to fry an egg," the woman screamed.

"I could have a hundred people lined up outside," the man bellowed, "and you'd tell me the cards said there ain't one in the crowd right for the job."

"The cards tell me what to do and they never lie. Never!"

The man came back outside, mopped his face with his apron, then turned and yelled back over his shoulder, "You know what you can do with those freaking cards."

Bishopp put his hand on my shoulder and told me to get back to the car. "You, too, Billy." He turned to Bertie. "This is no place for her."

Bertie and Billy led me back to the car, but before I got in, I called back to Bishopp. "I'm hungry. Starving."

Bertie gave me a push. "Get your behind in there." The car was hot and sticky, and when I complained Billy got out and opened all the doors. "That better?"

"No. And I'm still hungry."

Bertie told me to hush up in the voice she used when she was really aggravated, that I wasn't the only one who was hungry, and that as soon as Bishopp got directions to the gas station, we'd be on our way.

But we weren't. When Bishopp got back in the car, directions in hand, Billy turned the key. Nothing happened. He tried again. Still nothing. He tried twice more, then decided to give it a rest. "Must have flooded it."

The man stood watching all the while, and when Billy flicked the starter on one last time and still we sat, he walked over to the car, stuck his head in Bishopp's window, and said, "The kid said she was hungry." He looked from Bishopp to Bertie to Billy. "If one of you can sling hash, I got the eggs to go with it."

The Wizard at Work

14

A woman was sitting at a table in the corner of Rita's, shuffling a deck of cards. Mack called over to her. "Rita," he said, "this here is Bishopp. He's got problems. Big ones. His car overheated and his kid is hungry."

She shrugged.

"I'm gonna let Bertie"— he pointed to Bertie — "this here is Bertie . . . fix them some breakfast." He lifted a section of the counter to let Bertie go back to the kitchen. "Don't worry," he called back to Rita, "they'll pay."

He motioned for the rest of us to sit at the counter.

"Excuse me," Billy said. "Where's everybody?"

"Who everybody?"

"Truckers. There must be eight or ten trucks parked outside."

"I fool around with trucks. Used to fix them and sell them. But the cards told Rita I'd get in big trouble if I kept doing it. Something about state laws."

He turned his back to Rita and said in a loud whisper. "Ever since somebody made off with her fur coat, my wife lives by them cards." He sighed. "About twenty cooks ago, I had the extreme misfortune to hire somebody who happened to be a fortune-teller. You know how that changed my life?" He didn't wait for an answer. "Well, this little lady told the wife that she was gonna suffer a big loss AND, get this, she'd be divorced twice." He sighed again. "Since the coat is gone, she's waiting for me to take off with some little dandy." He looked back at Rita again and whispered, "Jealous of every lady that comes through that door."

He lifted up the counter again and went behind it. "You want a glass of milk, girlie?" Mack asked me.

"Please."

"How old are you?" he asked, giving me a glass of milk so full it dripped down on the counter.

"I'll be twelve September sixth," I said. "And thank you."

He waved his hand. *"Por nada,"* he said, smiling down at me. "That means 'for nothing' in Spanish. I learned that from the last cook I had." He laughed. "And that's what he did. Nothing.

"I could tell you stories about the cooks I've had like you wouldn't believe." He picked up a rag and started to wipe up the milk. "The fortune-teller not only showed the wife how to read cards, she taught her how to read heads."

I started to laugh.

"Yeah, I said heads. By the bumps." He lifted my hand and rubbed it on the front of his head. "Feel this? You know what this bump means?"

I shook my head.

"It means that I tend to have a mean and selfish nature." He dropped my hand. "I swear. The wife showed me the book." He reached for the rag again. "I don't think I have a mean and selfish bone in my body." He looked over toward Rita. "She don't use the heads much anymore. It's the cards. She don't go a day without them telling her when to get up and when to go to bed."

He turned and took some donuts out of a glass case and put them in front of me. "Help yourself. You, too," he said, looking over at Bishopp and Billy.

Before we could thank him, he said he had seven brothers, and what did we think about that. "Rita's got six, plus two sisters," he went on. "Funny, we got all those relatives and we never had a kid." He finished wiping the milk, put his hands on his hips, elbows flared, and nodded slowly. "Hey, don't misunderstand me. I'd do anything to have a kid, but Rita there, she's different." He turned to Bishopp. "How do you figure things?"

Without waiting for an answer, he said, "Well, I gotta call up some other agency to try to get me a cook. If I don't, I might as well close down for good." He looked over at Rita quickly, then bent down and whispered, "The eggs are on me."

More than eggs were on him. He gave Bertie some bacon to go with them and told her to use whatever she needed to make some biscuits. Billy brought in some raspberry jam from the trunk of the car, and when Bertie and Bishopp spread out the food, we said a quick prayer and ate.

"That was some good breakfast, Sister, and I thank you kindly," Billy said, drinking the last of his coffee. He stacked up the dishes and took them to the kitchen, then headed toward the door. "Now that she's had a chance to cool down, that old car will purr like a kitten when I start her up."

While Billy tried to get the car running, Bertie and I washed the dishes we'd used and Bishopp wiped down the counter. We were just about finishing up when Billy came in, shaking his head back and forth. "She won't start," he said. "I tried everything. She's dead, Bish. Just plain dead."

Bishopp looked as down as I'd ever seen him. He sat on one of the stools at the counter. "This is terrible. What are we going to do?"

"Pray," Bertie said. She was standing next to the sink, one of Mack's aprons around her waist, her arms folded high on her chest. "Hard."

I walked over to Bertie and put my arms around her. She hugged me to her and stroked my hair. "You don't worry none, sugar babe. Things are going to be just fine. You wait and see. Don't you be scared none."

I wasn't scared. In Bertie's arms, her hand stroking my hair, Bishopp and Billy right there, I almost felt like I was back home in Bertie's kitchen.

I started to pray. Not what Bertie and Bishopp and Billy were praying for. But I was praying. Hard.

Stairway to Paradise

15

$\mathcal{B}$ertie always told me that when you pray fervently, with your whole being, your prayer goes from your lips to God's ear. I never believed her, because most times what I prayed for didn't happen. Like praying that Gram would come out of the Shady Lawn Rest Home and be like Gram again. Or praying that my father would come to see me and tell me he loved me and wanted me. But now I kind of believed it went to God's ear, because what I was praying for came true so fast I thought I was dreaming.

Bertie had just poured herself another cup of coffee when Rita jumped up from where she was sitting, yelling, "Mack! Mack! You gotta see this. I never seen anything like it. It's a miracle."

Mack dropped the telephone and ran over to where she sat. I could see her pointing to the cards she had laid out on the table, telling Mack something about the king of hearts and the king of clubs. She pointed over to us. "I swear, Mack, they're all here. Even the kid." She hugged him. "And will you look at where the ten of hearts is?" she said, kissing him first on one cheek and then the other. "I tell you, Mack, honey, things are gonna change around here. We'll be home before you know it."

They talked back and forth, Rita pointing to the cards, Mack, his cigarette bobbing, waving his arms, their voices rising and falling. I could only catch bits and pieces, Mack asking what the queen of clubs had to do with Bertie, Rita saying something about the eight of clubs. "I'm telling you, it's a miracle." When she calmed down, they walked back to where we were.

"This here is the wife, Rita," Mack said.

"I am very happy to make your acquaintance," she said.

Mack asked us to please join them at the table where Rita had the cards laid out. When we got settled, he said, "Hey, what I'm gonna say is gonna sound crazy, but I'm gonna say it anyway." He took a deep breath. "Rita here claims that the cards tell her you people got more trouble than car trouble. She says you got serious financial trouble."

Bishopp started to speak, but Mack went right on, saying that he realized our personal troubles were none of his business, but since he was in trouble himself, what with the business going down because he couldn't keep a cook or a waitress, maybe a mutual arrangement could be made. He went on to say that every person who came through the door looking for a job had failed Rita's card test. Until today. "Hey," he said, leaning toward Bishopp, "she says you're all on the table. The kid is on twice." He turned to Rita. "Ain't that right?"

"It's like a miracle."

He looked over at Bertie. "What'd you think of you becoming a temporary cook here?"

Before Bertie could answer, Bishopp said, "That is a preposterous suggestion. And all of this card business is foolishness."

Rita's mouth fell, her eyes opened wide. "Excuse me," she said. "This is not foolishness." She pointed to the king of hearts. "Do you know what this card tells me?" She picked it up and put it under Bishopp's nose. "It tells me that a handsome, fair-complexioned, generous man has entered my life." She slapped the card back on the table. "Are you generous?"

"This is ridiculous," Bishopp said.

She ignored him and held up the queen and king of clubs. "This," she said, putting the queen of clubs in front of Bertie, "means that a warm, dark woman who is affectionate and helpful has entered my life." Bertie smiled.

"You never married, right?"

Bertie nodded.

Rita glanced over at Mack. "Didn't I tell you?" Without waiting for an answer, she turned to Billy and told him that his card represented a friendly and helpful man.

Billy looked a little puzzled at first, but then smiled and said, "Well, I like to think I'm friendly and helpful."

"The cards don't lie."

Rita put two cards in front of me. She picked up the seven of clubs. "This says you are a dark-haired girl who brings joy." She handed me the card. "Do you?"

I shrugged.

"She sure does," Bertie said, sounding as though she was getting into all this.

Bishopp shot her a glance.

"And this," Rita said to me, pointing to the eight of clubs, "tells me that someday you're gonna come into a fortune."

Bishopp started to get up, but Mack stopped him. Rita picked up the king of hearts again and put it in front of me. "Tell me something, hon. You think this card describes your hoity-toity friend over there?"

I knew Bishopp was generous and his hair had been light brown and was now gray, but I'd never thought of him like that. He was just Bishopp. My Bishopp. I looked at him. He was blushing a little. I'd never seen him do that either.

"This is nonsense," he said, again moving to get up.

"Just a minute," Rita said, pointing to the three tens surrounding Bishopp's card. "You want to know how I know you're in deep financial trouble?" She tapped her first finger on the table, her long red nail clicking in time to her words. "These told me and they're not wrong. I know that and so do you." She picked up the eight of hearts. "This tells me you're going on a long journey." She shook her head. "I see quarrels ahead."

Bishopp said that in no way did he believe in fortune-telling, that it was all coincidental, or could be deduced from just looking at us. "To stay here indefinitely is out of the question."

Mack shook his head and slapped his hands on the table. "Did I say forever? It's only temporary. Hey, look, your car's busted, and like Rita said, the cards say you need money." He leaned over toward Bishopp. "You could wait tables. I tell you, when word gets around that this place is going again, the truckers tip pretty good. I could even use the kid.

"And like I said, it's only temporary. I keep my business going, you get the repairman to fix your car, and you're on your way. Everybody's happy.

"When I put a sign up telling everybody I'm back in business, this place will be packed within ten minutes.

"Come on," Mack said, shifting around in his chair, "what've you got to lose. A few days? A week? I'm telling you, the repairman only works when he needs the dough. He ain't no Speedy Gonzales." He reached out for Rita's hand. "The wife ain't happy down here. She misses Brooklyn. I figure if I get a few good months, I can sell the place and we're out of here." He sighed. "Come on, what d'you say?"

Bishopp excused himself, asking Bertie to come along with him. I could see them through the window, Bishopp shaking his head, frowning; Bertie shrugging and nodding; their hands gesturing. I got up and ran out to where they stood. "Please, Bishopp. Please let's stay. You're so worried about money. We won't have

to pay for anything here. We'll be getting paid! Please."
My heart pounded. A few months, that's what Mack
had said. We could still be together.

Bishopp shook his head. "If we're very careful, we
can make it."

"But what about the car?" I said. "It won't start.
And I'll bet it's going to cost a lot to get it fixed."

"She's right about that," Bertie said.

Bishopp looked over at Bertie. "You can't cook
for a crowd. And I certainly am not capable of waiting
on tables of hungry truckers."

"I'll help," I said. "Billy, too. You'll see, Bishopp."

Bertie said it was up to Bishopp, and that she'd
manage.

And the next thing I knew, Mack was telling us
how sorry he was that there was only one room for the
four of us. "But it's a big one." He led us up two flights
of stairs and into a room, the room with the lace curtain. It drifted in and out of the window, wrapping
itself around the birdcage I'd seen.

The room was filled with boxes stacked in corners
and on top of a huge bed. Mounds of clothes were piled
on the two cots that were against the wall. The floor
was bare except for the dust balls that bounced along
in the breeze.

Mack apologized for the condition of the room,
telling us that Rita had lost all interest in doing anything
around the house. "You should see the rooms downstairs. They're worse."

Bertie said something about not believing anything could be worse and asked Mack to get her some clean cloths and ammonia. "I'm not resting until this room is ready for resting in."

Ready or not, I loved the room already. I loved the tiny violets on the wallpaper. I loved the way the walls slanted in, making the big room seem smaller and more friendly. I loved the faded, brown photographs on the walls. I loved the way the breeze lifted the curtain, holding it high, like a kite making its way to heaven. I loved the lonely birdcage. But most of all, I loved us all being together in a room we could call our own.

I thought about what Rita had said. About my coming into a fortune. That *had* to mean my father was rich. Maybe he'd pay for somebody to help Ginny Graham at the bakeshop, and Bertie and Billy really could stay with us. For the first time since we left home, thinking about my father didn't make me feel all sick inside.

I went over to the birdcage. There were seeds and dust on the bottom and a few feathers. "Where's the bird?" I asked.

"Hey," Mack said, "the wife won't allow a bird in the house. Says they bring bad luck."

"But there are feathers in here."

"My old bird. She got rid of him fast when she took up all this fortune-telling business." He looked over at the cage. "Too bad. He was a good bird. But good bird or not, out he went." He winked at me. "I better watch it."

All at once I felt sorry for Mack. I went over to where he was lifting the boxes from the bed to put them under the eaves.

"I'll help you," I said.

"We gotta fatten you up first," he said, huffing as he heaved another box from the bed. "You look like a strong wind would blow you right out that window."

"That's not true," I said, lifting one of the biggest boxes from the bed and carrying it over to the eaves.

"Hey," he said, smiling a big, wide smile, "you're okay." He handed me the box he was holding. "Like the saying goes, You can't tell a book by its cover."

Then the two of us cleared the boxes away, as Bertie scrubbed and Bishopp and Billy emptied the car.

After everything was in place, Mack asked Billy and Bishopp to drive with him to where we had seen the billboard for Rita's Restaurant. "I'm slapping a big 'We're Open For Business Again' on that sign. Like I said, by tomorrow morning, we'll be turning them away."

While they were gone, Bertie got out the clothesline. She pushed the cots over to one side of the room, the big bed to the other. She found two nails, stretched the clothesline across the room, and hung two sheets over it.

"This is theirs," she said, pointing to the two cots. She took my hand, lifted one of the sheets separating the room, and plunked herself down on the bed, pulling me down with her. "And this is ours, sugar babe."

Whatever Gets You Thru the Night

16

*B*ertie fell asleep as soon as her head hit the pillow. I couldn't sleep, and neither could Bishopp or Billy. Billy kept saying he was too wide for the cot, and Bishopp complained about the heat. They were both right. Not only was Billy too wide, but his feet hung over the end.

The breeze had disappeared and the curtains hung as though the lace had turned to stone.

Billy grunted and groaned for a long while and then annouced he was going to sleep in the car. "It's roomier than this," he said. Bishopp decided he was going downstairs to ask Mack for a fan. "This heat is not bearable."

I looked around the room. The moon was full and its light made shadows where the walls slanted. Bertie snored softly, tiny puffs coming each time she let out her breath. I thought about my room at home, thinking how quiet it must be. My bed smooth, not a wrinkle in it. My pillow fluffed all day and night. I thought about Gram at the Shady Lawn Rest Home. The Shady

Lawn where no trees grew, just patches of wild grass and weeds. I thought of Bertie's petunias and wondered if anybody would water them. And Bosendorfer, alone in Gram's tiny sitting room. No more rides from room to room. No more music.

I thought of Bertie's kitchen, Joe Cudjoe's voice trapped somewhere inside her old Philco. Bishopp's pantry, his polishing cloth hanging on the back of the door. The hanger, empty, where he always hung his linen jacket. The porch swing only moving when the wind picked up. Every inch of our house quiet and still.

Once when Billy stopped for gas, I'd found a phone in a restroom. I'd put some change into it and called our number back home. The operator came on and said, "At the customer's request, this line has been disconnected." It was as though somebody had cut the line connecting me to home.

I slipped out of bed and prayed with my whole being that the car would take forever to get fixed, and we'd stay here, knowing that even though my prayer may be going to God's ear, it was not what was going to be.

When I climbed back into bed, I snuggled next to Bertie and closed my eyes, but sleep wouldn't come. "Bertie," I whispered, longing for her company, "are you sleeping?"

"Not now," she said. "It's too hot."

"Bishopp went down to get a fan."

"This room needs more than a fan." She sighed.

"You try to get some sleep now. We've got a busy day ahead."

I put my arm around her. "You know what this room reminds me of, Bertie? The way you have the sheets hung up?"

"I sure don't."

"That movie we saw when we went to visit Gram."

"We saw lots of movies visiting with her." She sighed again. "Seems that's all they think old people can do." She turned onto her back. "Which one you speaking of, sweetie?"

"The one where the lady is hitchhiking —"

"That's bad." She turned and faced me. "You never do that. When I'm not there to remind you, you never do that. You promise me?"

I kicked the covers off me. "Remember they weren't married and they stayed in a motel, and he put up the blanket?"

"I remember." Bertie laughed until the bed shook. "Well, one thing's certain, I am no Claudette Colbert and Bishopp and Billy for sure aren't Clark Gable."

"Why did he do that?" I asked.

"Why did who do what?"

"The man in the movie. Why did he put the blanket up?"

"Same reason I did. For privacy. Ladies need privacy."

"But all he had to do was peek over the blanket."

"He was supposed to be a gentleman on his good behavior." She laughed. "But him being Clark Gable and all, he probably took a good peek." She reached out and put her hand on my leg. "We ought to get us some sleep."

But I couldn't, not because of the heat. Every time I closed my eyes, my mind would take me back home. "Bertie," I said, "do you think I'll ever live in our house again?"

She didn't answer.

"Bishopp promised I'd see Gram again, but sometimes I get scared that I won't. That the house will just disappear. Gram, too."

"Don't you worry none. Your gram is being taken care of. And that old house is able to take care of itself, folks living there or not."

I sat up. "Why do you always say that? 'Don't you worry none,'" I mimicked. "That's what you're always saying, like I'm a stone statue or something, like I can stop thinking about things. Well, I can't."

Bertie turned slowly toward me. "Oh, honey, I know you can't." She sat up and put her arm around me. "That's the trouble. You think too much. Always worrying about something. Always thinking that things are going to turn out bad."

She rocked me back and forth.

"Why do you have to go to Ginny's?" A sob escaped from somewhere inside me.

"Because that's where the Lord's leading me. And you got to learn to trust that He's leading you somewhere, too. Somewhere you belong, only you haven't come to it yet."

"Bishopp's staying with me. He said so."

"That's right. He won't leave till you get yourself settled."

That'll take forever, I wanted to say, but Bertie kept talking.

"Come on now," she said, gently tugging at me until we were both lying down again. She put her arm under my head. "You remember the story about how I met your grandma? How the two of us stayed in that beat-up hotel in New York? Like the Whistling Swan, only worse.

"And there I was, all eighteen years of me, waiting on tables so I could eat, waiting in lines for an audition so I could work at what I wanted to do. Your grandma going one way, me another every day. I guess things were bad, but we never thought they were."

I snuggled closer to Bertie, knowing she was doing what she always did to make me feel better. She put her hand on my head and, as though her fingers were feathers, she ruffled my hair. "I was up from Tuscaloosa to make my fortune. I was going to be the first black singer at the Met. And your grandma, why she was going to be the youngest Musetta the Met ever had." She laughed a tiny laugh.

"Neither one of us made it. Leastways, not the way we thought. Your grandma finally played Musetta in London when she was almost thirty. I never did get to sing at the Met," she lifted her head a bit and pointed her finger at me. "Not that I wasn't good enough, the Met just wasn't ready to think there were blacks good enough to belong on their stage." She stopped talking, looked over at me to see if I was still awake, and then went on. "Your grandma had her own ideas, too, about my people. She thought we only sang spirituals." She laughed hard. "Can you beat that? A smart lady like her. I straightened her out fast."

She sighed. "The Met might not have been ready for Alberta Hill, but some mighty fine places were." She was quiet for a while.

"You think I've spent my life regretting any of it? No sir. My life's been good." She held her hand up, and in the dim light I could see her two fingers entwined. "Your grandma and I are still like this. Always will be." She sighed a long, sad sigh. "I miss her. But I truly believe the Lord will bring us together again, just like He did all those years ago. You just got to trust in Him." She gave me a squeeze. "And yourself."

"I love you, Bertie."

"And I love you, sugar babe." She pulled me closer. "You tired now?"

I wasn't, but I knew she was, so I said good night.

She kissed me. "Things are going to be fine. You'll see."

I lay back and thought about what Bertie had said. I wanted to believe that everything was going to be all right, but it was hard. I tried to forget what Bertie had said about Bishopp staying with me just for a while. But part of me wouldn't let me forget. I'd need him forever, but would he stay with me forever? I wished I knew for sure. "Rita," I said, sitting up. "Maybe she'll know." Bertie stirred beside me. I lay back.

Maybe Rita would know more. Maybe she'd know if my father would like me. Or want me. Maybe she could tell me lots of things I wanted to know.

I must have fallen asleep, because I had the strangest dream. In it, I heard somebody coming up the stairs.

"Bishopp?" I called out. "Is that you?"

"No, Phoebe," Bishopp's voice answered. "It's Pete."

"Pete?" I said in my dream.

"That's what I said. Just plain old Pete."

Magical Mystery Tour

17

"*B*ertie," I mumbled, reaching over to her side.

But I was alone in bed, and alone in the room. The only sound was coming from the fan Bishopp must have put in the window. I stretched and yawned, then decided to get up and get dressed. Somebody had taken the sheets down from the clothesline and sun lit up the room.

My suitcase was on the floor next to the bed. I yanked out some shorts and a top and dressed quickly. I rummaged in the bag for my sneakers, ran a comb through my hair, and headed downstairs. When I got to the landing, I heard strange voices, and the smell of bacon and coffee filled the air. Dishes rattled and music played so loud I could feel it thump in my chest. The restaurant was crowded. People, mostly men, filled the seats at the counter. The tables were full, too, and there were a few people waiting to be seated. Mack was stationed midway between the kitchen and the counter, his cigarette hanging from his mouth, his hat perched on his head. Bishopp was standing at a table, a pad in his hand, writing something down. He must have borrowed some of Mack's clothes, because I had never seen Bishopp dressed the way he was. White pants and a white shirt with the sleeves rolled up. And sneakers. Bishopp didn't own sneakers. He always wore shiny black oxfords.

I walked slowly toward the kitchen. Bertie was standing at the stove, flipping pancakes. "Soon as I finish with these orders," she called out to me, "I'll fix you some French toast." She had a huge white apron wrapped around her and she was wearing a hat like Mack's.

Billy was cracking eggs into a bowl, a hat on his head, too. "Morning, Phoeb."

Mack called over a good morning. "Didn't I tell you once that open-for-business sign went up, the crowd would come back?"

"He's like a record that got itself stuck in the same groove," Bertie muttered. She smiled at me. "You sleep okay?" Before I could answer, Mack yelled, "Three orders of hotcakes for table five, Bertie."

Bertie turned back to the grill, and motioned with her elbow to a table in the corner that was filled with glasses of orange juice. "Have your juice, Phoebe."

"There's milk in the refrigerator," Mack said, grinning over at me. "You help yourself to anything you want."

I sat at a table next to the refrigerator and watched. Right away I noticed Bertie's ankles were swollen.

Bishopp's face was flushed and he looked flustered. I felt bad. I hadn't realized how many people Bertie would have to cook for and how many tables Bishopp would have to serve. Bishopp wrote something down, erased it, held his ear close to the man who was talking to him, nodded, then wrote something else down. He turned toward Mack and said in a loud voice, "Two bull's-eyes, double the pig, and burnt tombstones, three times."

"You're catchin' on," Mack said, taking the unlit cigarette out of his mouth and putting it behind his ear as though it were a pencil. "I told you. You're a natural.

"Did you get that?" Mack called over to Bertie. "That's three orders of eggs, sunny-side up, double orders of ham, and well-done toast."

Bishopp burst into the kitchen and without as much as a good morning to me went over to a huge urn, filled three mugs with coffee, put them on his tray, and hurried back to the table where three men waited.

The clock on the wall said it was only nine o'clock, but it looked as though Bertie and Bishopp and Billy had been working at Rita's forever. Bertie's face glistened with sweat, Billy's, too. Bishopp kept wiping his face with his sleeve. I'd never seen him sweat before. Back home the temperature could reach 120 degrees and Bertie and I would be streteched out on the porch swing, trying to catch a breeze from the river. Gram would be up in her room, shades drawn, drinking iced tea, holding the icy glass against her cheeks when she thought nobody was looking. Miss Jean would take to her bed, ice pack on her head; Billy would go down to the damp, cold basement to do his chores. Only Bishopp would "carry on," as he used to say, cool as always.

Bertie kept calling over to me to be patient, that the French toast was coming, but it never did. Mack kept calling egg and pancake orders in to her. When things began to quiet down, she brought me a plate of pancakes and sausage. She had just about put them in front of me when another crowd came through the door. Everybody flew around again. Bertie flipped pancakes, Billy cracked eggs, and Bishopp scurried from table to table, people yelling out to him for more coffee.

It hadn't been a dream last night. Bishopp *was* Pete. "Fill me up, Pete," they'd call, holding up their coffee mugs. When I asked Bertie why they were doing that, she told me that Mack said nobody would appreciate having to call a waiter Bishopp, especially in a place like Rita's. "Too formal," he'd said. "This place is definitely not into formality." He'd asked Bishopp what his first name was, then decided even Peter was too formal for Rita's place. "You're Pete here. Okay with you?"

Well, it wasn't with me. I didn't like seeing him dressed the way he was, either, his feet all queer looking in sneakers; his shirtsleeves rolled up to his elbows, baring his pale, thin arms. Bishopp, who was always dressed in his black pants and his creamy-white linen jacket, didn't look like himself. And people calling him Pete wasn't respectful.

I didn't like Bertie standing at a big stove fixing pancakes for a million people, either. I didn't like seeing her in white wearing a hat in the kitchen. It made me think of how Miss Jean always wanted Bertie to dress in a black uniform with a tiny maid's cap on her head when she was around. I told Bertie she should take the hat off. Billy, too. But she said that Mack would be in trouble if the Board of Health representative came in for an inspection. "It's the law, sweetie. Cooks got to have their hair covered."

Billy shrugged and kind of grinned at me. "The law's the law, Phoeb." He looked silly, as silly as the lady wearing the pink ribbon at the Shady Lawn Rest Home.

Now I really felt terrible for begging them the way I did to stay.

I tried helping Bertie, reminding her that Mack said I was to work, too, but she told me she was too busy to tell me what to do, though when lunchtime came she'd need me. "Why don't you go on up and read? Or write a nice, long letter to your grandma."

I *had* been writing a letter to my grandmother in my head. I used to write like that to my father. But when I got to writing it down, I'd get as far as "Dear Father, no . . . Dear Daddy, no . . . Dear Dad —" Nothing seemed right, so I'd go on writing in my head. And now it was the same way with my grandmother. "Dear Gram," I'd write. "I miss you . . ." And then I'd stop. I'd even stopped writing in my diary because ever since everything began to change, whatever I wrote in my diary made me sad.

I headed toward the stairs leading to our room, but Rita was sitting at a table near the exit, and when I passed I stopped and said good morning to her.

"Sit down," she said. "Have some coffee."

"No thank you," I said, sitting myself across from her. "I don't like coffee."

She rolled her eyes. "I'd be dead without it."

I must have looked puzzled because she explained that she had a hard time waking up in the morning. "Mack brings me a pot of strong coffee, and by the time I'm finished I'm ready for anything. Sounds crazy, but it works."

She shuffled the deck of cards she was holding. "Back home in Brooklyn that's the way my father woke up." She made two piles of cards, put her thumbs at the bottom of each, and snapped the two piles into one. "You know Brooklyn at all?"

I shook my head.

"Boy, do I miss it." She tapped the cards on the table and put the pack down. "Where you from?"

"Lubelle County," I said. "You know where that is?"

She shook her head. "We've been living here for seven years and don't know the name of the next town." She patted the cards. "But I know a lot about people." She leaned toward me. Her breath smelled queer, like cough medicine. "Except I don't know your name."

"Phoebe. My real name is Dominique Phoebe Howland Fiore, but I've always been known as Phoebe."

"That's quite a mouthful. Who's the Dominique after?"

"My father."

"Ahhh," she said, fanning the cards on the table, picking up several cards. "I've been wondering why I keep coming up with the same card and it's always next to you." She held up the seven and eight of clubs in her right hand. "These are you. Remember?"

She didn't wait for an answer. She held up the jack of clubs in her left hand. "Could be your father," she said in a singsong voice.

"Why do you think that?"

"I said, 'could.' I'd have to do a reading before I know for sure."

"What's a reading?"

"A reading tells what's going to happen in the future. Just like when you came and the cards told me exactly who was who and you had money troubles. Remember?"

Again, she didn't let me answer.

"I do my own personal reading every morning. This morning it wasn't too good. I got two eights next to Mack's card."

"Why wasn't that good?"

"Are you serious? Two eights next to the king of diamonds, which is Mack, means trouble and arguments. So today I stay away from him." She looked over toward him. "See how happy he is? If I went over and talked to him, he'd change"— she snapped her finger in the air — "just like that. Why, we'd be in a fight if I as much as said good morning." She leaned back. "The cards don't lie."

"Just from the cards you can tell that?"

She nodded. "I'll prove it to you."

She got up and went over to where Mack was, kissed him, and said a loud "Good morning." All of a sudden, Mack was yelling something about how it's only nine o'clock in the morning and look at you. Then he raised his hands and said, "For God's sake, Rita, will you lay off of it?"

She turned and pranced back to the table.

"See?" she said, laughing and flopping back into the chair. "I kiss him, say a nice 'good morning,' and look what happens. A fight as soon as I open my mouth."

She clicked her fingernails on the cards. "These do not lie, sweetie pie. They. Do. Not. Lie."

Bishopp had said it was all ridiculous and foolish, but I saw it with my own eyes. All she did was kiss Mack and say good morning, and there it was: trouble.

"Do you think you could tell my fortune, Rita?"

She sighed. "I charge," she said, her voice low. "I could do a quick palm reading, or I could read the bumps on your head for free, but the cards — no." She leaned over toward me and said in a heavy whisper, "See, it's like this. The wonderful Gypsy lady who taught me how to do this made me promise I would never do it for nothing. Like she said, and it's true, what you get for nothing, means nothing. Understand?"

I nodded. "How much do you charge?"

"How much have you got?" She leaned closer. "This is just between you and me. Okay?"

"Okay. But I've only got about three dollars."

"That's all?"

I nodded again. "But Mack said I'd get paid when I start helping Bertie in the kitchen. I could pay more then."

"So you pay me the three dollars when I do the reading and the rest when Mack pays you."

"How much is the rest?"

"Depends on the reading. Probably for you about six dollars total." Her voice dropped to a whisper. "Remember, you don't say nothing to nobody about the money."

I thought she'd start reading my cards right then, but she said she couldn't do that. Had to get prepared, she said. Set up her table. Be in the mood. "I have to rest before I do a reading," she said, her palms pressed against her head, her eyes closed. "I have to be in touch with the psychic energy that flows from the cards, through my hands, and into my consciousness." She opened her eyes. "Maybe later, hon."

She flipped through the cards. "But I'll tell you what the cards told me already." She held up the ten of spades. "An important letter is going to come into your hands. Maybe you got it already." She leaned forward.

"Are you a worrier?" As usual, she didn't let me answer. She held up the three sevens. "See these?" She laughed. "A baby is in your future. Maybe your mother?"

"My mother is dead."

She stopped laughing, her face serious. "I'm sorry, hon. I'm really sorry." She gathered all the cards up from the table. "Maybe your father? Is he married again?"

"I don't know."

"Maybe you?" she said, laughing a tiny laugh.

I didn't answer her.

She shrugged, flipped the cards once more, and said, laughing a big laugh, "Well, as long as it ain't yours truly." Then she put the cards into a small box, stuffed them into her skirt pocket, and was gone.

Things Are Changing

18

*W*hen I got up to the top of the stairs I felt so different. Ever since Gram had gotten sick and there was talk of us taking this journey to find my father, I had felt powerless over everything. Thoughts would spin around in my head, always making me afraid of what was going to happen. Whenever I told Bertie about it, she'd go on about my being with old folks too much, and that what I needed were friends my own age. "A child your age worrying the way you do, it's just not right," she'd say. But as hard as I tried not to worry, the thoughts didn't stop.

Now, though, I had hope. I didn't care if Bishopp thought it was ridiculous, or Bertie thought Rita was foolish; the cards *did* mean something. Hadn't they told Rita about us? About our money problems? Didn't I see with my own eyes what happened when she went over to Mack to say good morning?

I fished my money from my suitcase and stuffed it into my pocket. I wasn't going to tell anybody about the reading. Not even Billy. He didn't think Rita was crazy. He kind of liked what the cards said about him.

The more I thought about the reading, the more excited I got. Imagine my father appearing in the cards. Me coming into a fortune. And the letter. How could she have known about the letter, the one that said my father would do anything for Gram and me?

"What are you looking so happy about, sweet thing?"

I looked up and there was Bertie standing in the doorway of our room, the white apron still wrapped around her, the hat on her head.

"I'm going to put this body in a horizontal position for a while," she said. "My feet are killing me, and Mack tells us the supper crowd will start up at three."

She stretched out on the bed. "What you been doing?"

"Nothing."

"Well, that's going to change come two o'clock. I'll need some help in the kitchen." She yawned a big, wide yawn. "Did you write to your gram?"

"No. I'll do it tonight."

She pulled the spread over her. "If I fall asleep, make sure you wake me. You hear?"

"I hear."

"And make sure you write that letter. Livia'll be glad to hear from you."

"She probably won't even know it's from me."

"Maybe she will, maybe she won't. But that doesn't mean you don't write."

She turned, breathed a deep sigh, and then slept,

the clatter of the fan drowning out the soft put-put-put of her snoring.

I crept noiselessly out of the room and down the stairs. I had decided to give Rita all the money I had, which came to almost four dollars. I figured if I did, she'd be more inclined to tell me when she'd do the reading. Maybe she'd do it now. But when I got down to the restaurant, it was empty. A sign on the counter said, "GONE FISHING — BE BACK IN TEN MINUTES."

I went out to the parking lot. Gram's car wasn't there and neither was Mack's truck. That meant Bishopp and Billy had taken the car over to the gas station to get it fixed. I said a quick prayer asking God to make sure the repairman didn't have the urge to work today. Then I decided I should make a list of questions to ask Rita at my reading. She probably charged by the time she took, and if I had all the questions ready it wouldn't cost as much.

I sat at a picnic table and started the list.

"Questions to Ask at Phoebe's Reading"

1. Will Bishopp stay with me?
2. Will my grandmother get better?
3. Will we find my father?'
4. If we do find my father, will he be rich?
5. Will he let Bishopp stay? And Bertie and Billy?
6. Why did he leave my mother and me?

I stopped writing, afraid to ask the next question. What if the cards said no? No, he doesn't love you. No, he doesn't want you. I thought about the letter he'd written to Gram saying he'd never love anybody as he had loved my mother. I knew from books I'd read that some people only love one person in their entire life. I'd asked Bishopp if that was true, and he said he believed it to be true, that some people never loved anybody. "My father, to my knowledge, didn't. Certainly he never showed love to my mother. Nor to me, or any child that followed. Not even as babies."

My stomach began to twitch. I thought about the baby Rita had told me about. Maybe my father had married again. Maybe he did have a baby. Or more. If he did, maybe he wouldn't even have room for Bishopp and me in his house.

I stuffed the list in the pocket with my money and went back inside. Rita was back at her table, the cards before her. I raced over, reached into my pocket, and placed the money on the table. "It's almost four dollars," I said.

"What?" I smelled that same queer odor coming from her.

"I said, it's almost four dollars. I told you I had only three, but I found more."

She looked up at me, confused. "What are you talking about?"

"My reading. You said this morning you'd do my reading and that it would be about six dollars."

"I did?"

I nodded. "Can you do it now?"

She sighed and shook her head. "What did you say I told you?"

"That there was a baby in my future. You even told me about an important letter —"

"You sound like Mack." Before I could ask why, she said, "He's always telling me I say things I didn't say."

My whole body sagged, and try as I did, I couldn't stop my eyes from filling up. "Please, Rita, please do my reading. I need to know things."

"Okay. Okay," she said, reaching out for the money, "only stop blubbering." She tucked the money into her blouse. "One thing I can't stand is blubbering." She pushed away from the table. "I'll see if I can work you in."

"When?"

"Try me later."

"Phoebe," Bertie's voice boomed from the kitchen, "you get your behind on in here as fast as you can move yourself."

"Okay. Okay," I yelled back. I turned to Rita. "What time?"

"Don't you go okaying me. You get on in here. NOW."

Rita waved me off. "Later," she mumbled.

"PHOEBE!"

I thanked Rita and ran into the kitchen.

"Next time I tell you to wake me, you be sure you do just that." Bertie tied an apron around me, plunked a hat on my head, and told me to get busy with the carrots and the potatoes. "Slice them real thin so's they cook fast. We're running out of time."

Come into My Parlor . . .
19

The afternoon flew by. I peeled and sliced a thousand carrots, and at least that many potatoes, but I don't remember doing it. I guess while my body was in Mack's kitchen, my mind was off to Lubelle County and somewhere on an island in Maine.

Bishopp and Mack came back in time to help with the supper crowd. Billy had stayed with the car. Seems the repairman hadn't showed up for work. The owner of the station had said it was highly unusual for him to be late and that he'd definitely be in by early afternoon.

"Highly unusual my foot," Mack said when he came into the kitchen. "I've heard that same story a million times. Far as I'm concerned, and I told Billy, if he ain't there in the morning, he sure as hell won't be there in the afternoon."

Bertie told him to mind his mouth.

Mack apologized. "Keep forgetting I've got ladies around."

Bishopp kept racing back and forth to the kitchen,

filling coffee mugs, yelling orders to Bertie. I couldn't believe it. This morning they'd looked terrible. And now Bishopp, who never raised his voice to Bertie back home, and Bertie, who would have put Bishopp "in his place" if he did, seemed to be enjoying themselves. Bertie filled plate after plate, Bishopp tossed rolls and butter on top of Bertie's stew or meatloaf or whatever and hurried back to the dining room.

When the last of the supper crowd was fed, Bishopp came into the kitchen and fell into a chair, exhausted. He said his body was so stiff he couldn't bend to take off the daft things he had on his feet. I ran over and untied the laces, slipped the sneakers off, and began to rub his feet the way I sometimes did for Bertie.

"Aaaaah," he said, "good as that feels, you don't have to do that."

"I want to."

"Thank you," he said. "Makes me think I'd better wear my shoes tomorrow. Those things have no support."

"You don't look like yourself in them," I said. "And I don't like it when they call you Pete."

"Peter's my given name. Quite a nice name."

I tried to explain that it wasn't that I didn't like the name Peter, it was the way everybody yelled "Pete" out at him and the way he ran around serving them like he was always just Pete, the waiter at Rita's Restaurant.

"Phoebe," he said gently, "people must adapt to situations that are forced upon them."

I knew that. I saw that with my own eyes. The

way he joked around with the customers, making them laugh.

"It's not dignified," I said.

He laughed and reached down and took my face in his hands. "Even if it makes me feel younger and less like an old fogy?" I didn't answer him. I wanted him to stay the way he was. I was afraid if he changed, things would change with him.

He gave my face a squeeze and said, "What did you do to keep yourself occupied today?"

"Helped Bertie. Didn't you see me?"

"Can't say that I did, it got so busy."

"I did the carrots and the potatoes."

"Well, that I figured out for myself," he said in a loud whisper. "Bertie is not known for her dainty slices."

"I heard that," Bertie said, sitting down beside him, a smile on her face, "but I'm too tired to let it bother me." She looked over at me. "I put some hot dogs on. How about you fixing them up?"

I was happy to do it. It made me feel good to do things for them. Mack came over and sat with us when the hot dogs were ready. I had put some of Bertie's relish on the table, and when Mack tasted it, he announced that starting tomorrow, the supper special at Rita's Restaurant would be: "Three Bertie dogs, a side of spuds, and an ice-cold, foaming root beer."

As soon as he finished, he said he had to go check up on something and that as soon as Bishopp was ready, he'd take him over to the gas station to pick up Billy.

"That man's sure got his sack of rocks to carry," Bertie said to Bishopp as soon as Mack was out of sight.

Bishopp nodded.

Bertie never said anybody had troubles. They either had a sack of rocks to carry or a mountain to climb. If they had really huge troubles, they had a cross to carry.

Before I could ask her why Mack had a sack to carry, she looked over at me. "I've got a bone to pick with you, child. You remember I told you to call me at two?"

"I was just going up to call you when you called me —"

"You could have fooled me, the way you were yackety-yacking with Rita. What was that all about?"

"She was telling me how she learned to read cards."

"Don't you go believing that those cards can tell you what's coming."

"But —"

"No buts." Bertie looked over at Bishopp. "I don't want this child's head filled with a bunch of nonsense."

Bishopp said that Bertie was absolutely right and that he would prefer that I not spend too much time with Rita. "She is a troubled lady."

"You're just saying that because of what Bertie said."

"Is that a fact?" Bertie said. She went on to say

that between her and Bishopp, they had lived well over a hundred years and that they hadn't spent it sleeping. "We have learned a thing or two along the way. Besides," she said, smiling over at Bishopp, "anything that Mr. Hoity-Toity and I agree on has got to be true."

I knew better than to argue, seeing as the two of them were on the same side. I helped Bertie clear up and then all of us worked on the dishes and pots and pans from supper. When the tables had been set up for breakfast, we were finished for the day.

Bishopp asked me if I wanted to drive over to get Billy with Mack and him, but I told him I thought I'd write a letter to Gram. He looked pleased and asked me to give Gram his best. As always, my chest got that heavy feeling.

Bertie headed on up to our room. "I'm going to take a nice, long bath," she said. "And even though the sun's got a way to go, I'm putting this body to bed." She reminded me at least three times to write to Gram. "And don't you go seeking Rita out. You hear?"

I shook my head and got ready for the heavy feeling again. It came, because as soon as Bishopp and Mack were out the door and I'd checked to make sure Bertie was asleep, I made my way up to the second-floor apartment where Mack and Rita lived. I knocked on the door and waited. No answer. I knocked again. And again. I was just about to leave when I heard Rita's voice. "Who is it?"

"It's me."

"Who?"

"Phoebe."

She opened the door, a coffee cup in her hand. "Yeah?" she said, pushing her hair away from her face. She was wearing a long, blue fuzzy robe that was wrinkled and stained. She looked as though she'd just gotten out of bed.

"Don't you feel well?" I asked.

She shrugged. "I feel okay. Just a little tired." She kind of shifted back and forth. "You want something?"

"My reading. You said you'd do it today."

"Oh, yeah," she said. "Today."

I nodded. "Can you do it now? Please?"

She started to shake her head, but then shrugged. "What the heck," she said, opening the door just enough to let me pass. "Get in and let's get this over with."

. . . Said the Spider to the Fly

20

The room was dark and smelled musty, as though no air ever came in. "Excuse the looks of the place. I'm in the process of redecorating."

"I thought you and Mack were moving back to Brooklyn soon."

"He's been saying that for seven years. Never happen."

She motioned me over to a small table in the corner. A dark green light hung over the table. The glass shade was cracked, making it look like a small bolt of lightning had passed through. A dark gray cat sat under the table, sharpening his claws on the carpet.

"Go sit down," Rita said.

I crept over to the chair and slid onto it, careful not to disturb the cat. As soon as I got settled it leapt up onto my lap. I stiffened.

"Relax. She always does that when she's in the family way." Rita took the seat opposite me. "Just sit still, that way she won't get nervous.

"I thought it was a he," I said. "It's so big."

"You'd be big too if you were going to have six or seven babies."

I asked her how she knew the cat was having so many kittens, but she paid no attention. She excused herself and went back to the kitchen. The cat purred in my lap. After a while, Rita came back into the room and sat down again.

"Okay, now," she said, "I'm going to do what we call the Mystic Star." Rita took out the queen of diamonds and held it up. "This is what we call the client card. In other words, it's you —"

"But you told me I was the seven and eight of clubs."

"Oh," she said, "that's right. Sorry." She took out the eight of clubs. "Only one client card to a reading." She put the card in the middle of the table.

She pushed the rest of the deck toward me. "Shuffle."

I did and passed it back to her.

"Now cut it twice.

"Not with your right hand." She took the pack back. "The left hand. You always use the left hand." She handed the pack back to me. "Now shuffle again."

"Okay, now, cut it twice . . . that's right, the left hand." She leaned back in her chair. "The mystic forces won't flow through the right.

"Now make three piles.

"Not faceup," she said, her voice on edge. "Facedown.

"Okay, we're ready."

She turned the cards right-side up. "Hmmmmnnn, three sevens again." She looked right through me as though she were alone in the room. "I don't understand why that baby keeps floating around here. Makes me crazy."

"Maybe it's because the cat is having kittens."

She leaned over to me, her eyes wide, that same queer smell still with her. "Who's doing this, you or me?"

"Sorry."

"I do readings for people, not cats. And another thing, I need to concentrate. You say one more word and you're out of here. Understand?"

I nodded and forced a tiny smile, afraid she would put me out before I found out what she already knew.

She passed me the cards and told me to shuffle them again.

"Now for the star," she said, counting out three cards, laying them facedown around the eight of clubs, until all the cards, in piles of three, were on the table forming a star shape.

"I'm ready to begin." One by one she took each pile, turned it over, and studied the cards. After a while, she got up, went into the kitchen, and came back with a glass in her hand. She took a long drink, then picked up a pile of cards.

She sat very still. Rigid almost. She closed her eyes and put her hands on the jack of clubs. After a long time, she said very softly, "I don't understand."

She opened her eyes, fanned the cards out, and stared

down at the three cards before her. She put her right palm over the jack of clubs, held her left hand up, and closed her eyes again. "Come on. What's with this baby? Tell me what I need to know. Who is this?"

I wanted to leap up and shout, "It's my father. You said so this morning." But all I did was stroke the cat's fur.

Rita took the card, her eyes still closed, and placed it on her forehead. "Everything seems clouded. He keeps fading.

"Yes," she said, nodding, "I understand that, but what's he hiding from?"

Again I wanted to shout out that it was my father and it was me he was hiding from, but I didn't dare move, I just kept stroking the cat.

Rita sighed and nodded, and after a long while, opened her eyes, scooped the cards from the table, and said, "Something's not right here. I'm finished —"

"But you promised you'd do it." The cat leapt from my lap into hers.

"Look what you did," Rita said, her voice sharp. "Poor little thing is shaking." She nuzzled her face into the cat's fur. "That's okay, Powder Puff, Mommy's here." Rita looked over at me. "I said, that's it."

"I paid you!" I shouted, jumping up from my chair. "You told me if I paid you you'd tell me what was going to happen."

"Keep your damn mouth shut," she hissed. She got up, the cat under her arm, her drink in her hand, and walked toward the door. She opened it as wide as she had when she let me in. "Sometimes it's better not to know," she said in a suddenly sweet voice. "Trust Rita, sweetie."

I pleaded, but she dismissed me with her silence. I walked past her, toward the stairs leading to our room.

I heard a door open behind me and thought it might be Rita calling me back. But it was Mack coming out of the room he stored canned goods in. "What was that all about? I heard Rita yelling about something."

"Nothing," I said.

He came over to me and put his arm around me. "Rita sometimes gets into moods. Don't let it get to you. She gets moody being alone all the time. You know what I mean?"

I shrugged.

"I keep telling her what we need is a kid." He looked down at me. "One like you." Then he bent down and kissed the top of my head, and when he did, the door to their apartment swung open. Rita stood in the doorway. "Hey!" she yelled. "You just wait a minute."

I turned, thinking that she had changed her mind, that she would go on with the reading, that she *hadn't* seen something she wouldn't tell me about.

"I'm warning you," she said, her voice a harsh whisper. "Quit making goo-goo eyes at my husband, or you won't have a future to worry about."

Mack told me to get on upstairs, then told Rita to shut her mouth and went into the room and closed the door behind them.

A Dandelion Dies in the Wind

21

"And don't come back! You hear me?"

Bertie's suitcase came flying out the window, her clothes going one way, her shoes another. Bishopp's came out next.

"What's the matter with you?" Mack yelled from beneath the window. "You gone crazy or something?"

"Crazy, am I? I'll show you how crazy I am!"

Rita leaned out of the window of what once was our bedroom, the lace curtain draped over her head, and dropped my suitcase. It hit the porch roof and popped open. Pants and tops and underwear floated down. Papers fluttered like dried leaves and dropped all over the parking lot.

Bishopp and Bertie and I ran around catching what we could. "Get going," Rita bellowed, aiming my old diary at me. "And take Little Miss Goo-Goo Eyes with you."

"See here, now," Bishopp said, looking up at Rita, "that's no way to talk."

Rita's hands gripped the sill, her head and shoulders hanging out. "I'll talk any damn way I please, Mr. Hoity-Toity. This is my room. My house. My restaurant. My parking lot."

She turned and Billy's suitcase came flying through the window and landed at Bertie's feet. Sneakers, shoes, Bertie's bras, Bishopp's pants sailed through the air. The last thing to hit the ground was the clothesline Bertie had strung up. "You know what you can do with this?" Rita shouted. "Hang yourselves."

Mack ran into the house and within seconds was at the window with Rita.

He tried to pull her back, but she pushed him away.

"What are you doing?" he shouted. "What's the matter with you?"

"What's the matter with *me?*" she shouted back. "It's not me that something's the matter with. It's you and that little twit —"

"Shut your mouth," Mack yelled, yanking Rita back.

"Get them out of here," she yelled. "Now."

"You better calm down," Mack yelled back, "or they'll take you out of here in a straight jacket." He slammed the window shut.

Even with the window shut, their voices muffled, I could hear Rita screaming over and over, "Get them out."

Bertie and Bishopp stood staring up at the window, puzzled. I did, too, but I wasn't puzzled. I knew what it was all about. My reading. I'd kept it a secret

141 🦋

from everybody. I'd have told Billy if he'd given me the opportunity, but as soon as he finished helping with the supper crowd, he'd take off for the gas station, even though the repairman hadn't shown up yet.

Instead I'd lain beside Bertie for four nights wanting to reach out to her to spill it all out. I'd kept guard on Bishopp, afraid that maybe something terrible was going to happen to him, that that was the awful thing the cards had told Rita. I'd slip out of bed and sit on the floor where I could see Bishopp's sheet rise and fall until my eyes refused to stay open. But once back in bed, it came back to my father. It was my father she couldn't tell me about. He didn't want me. He was hiding from me and always had. And when I finally slept, I would dream the dream I often had. But different. Bertie and Billy are gone.

I am in that same field filled with dandelions. My father is waiting for me in that same clearing. Bishopp gathers an armful of the yellow flowers and places them in my arms. Pleased and happy, I run toward my father, but when I get to the clearing, he disappears. I look around and he waves to me from across the field. I race to him, but he is gone when I get there. Again and again, he comes and goes. Again and again I run toward him until all of the flowers, those Bishopp has picked and those he has left, are trampled beneath my feet.

"Lord God Almighty, what is this all about?"

The sound of Bertie's voice brought me back to the parking lot.

Bishopp reached out and put his arm around her. "I think the cards told her something. And I think we're going to be on our way."

He looked over at me. "Better gather up what we can, Phoebe. She means business."

Bertie got the suitcases lined up and we began picking clothes from bushes, shoes from Mack's truck, and whatever else Rita had thrown out. Bertie shook her head each time she picked something up and put it in its owner's suitcase. "That lady's got one big mountain to climb," she said, tossing one of Billy's shoes into his case.

"So do we, Bertie," Bishopp said, heading toward some papers that had blown against the porch. My stomach tightened. In all the excitement I'd forgotten about my papers, the letter telling where my father was. I dropped the mate of Billy's shoe and raced toward the papers, gathering them up before Bishopp could.

"Just put them in one of the bags for now. We can sort them out later," he said.

Once they were safely at the bottom of my suitcase, my clothes concealing them, we gathered up what remained. When the last of our belongings were tucked into the suitcases, we sat at the picnic bench to wait for Mack. Bishopp thought Mack might agree to drive us to the gas station. "Perhaps the car will be ready."

"That would be a miracle," Bertie said.

Bishopp sighed and said he hoped that would be the case. But I knew he didn't believe it.

The sun was high, the breeze had died, and the air was still. Only the sound of Rita's voice broke the stillness. It came closer. The front door swung open and there she was, a box at her feet. She bent down, picked up two jars of Bertie's relish, and threw them, splattering them on the black tar of the parking lot.

Bertie started to get up, but Bishopp held her back. "Let Mack take care of this."

Mack appeared in the doorway and pulled Rita back into the house, slamming the door behind them. We sat until the sun was low in the sky before Mack came out again. He walked slowly over to us. "I'm sorry," he said.

He turned to Bishopp and asked if he could have a word with him. Bertie and I waited, and when they came back, it had been decided that Mack would drive us to the gas station.

We piled our belongings into the back of one of his pickup trucks. Bertie sat up in the cab with Mack. Bishopp and I rode in the back.

"What did Mack say?" I asked, wanting to know if he had told Bishopp my reading had caused all of this.

"That Rita is sick."

"She didn't look sick, the way she was throwing things at us."

"Not physically sick."

"Like Gram?"

He shook his head. "We'll talk about it later," he said, his voice weary.

He looked so tired it scared me. I wanted to put his head in my lap as he'd done to me so many times, to smooth his hair and tell him everything would be all right. But his all right wasn't my all right.

Bishopp leaned back and closed his eyes as Mack's truck roared up the road. The breeze whipped my hair across my face and stood Bishopp's up, like he'd been electrocuted. When the truck came to a final stop, I was the one who had to shake Bishopp awake.

The Child Stands Alone

22

"Hey there," Billy said, grinning and heading on over to the truck when he spotted us, "what's all this?"

He waved in to Mack and Bertie, then came back to where Bishopp and I were. "What are you all doing here?"

He leaned against the side of the truck, motionless, as Bishopp explained what had happened.

"You mean that's it? We're out of there?" He leaned over toward Bishopp. "Then we're in big trouble. That repairman showed up a while back, took one look at the car, and said it'd take a month of Sundays just to get the parts to fix her up. The main drive shaft is gone. It's going to cost. Big."

Bishopp sighed and hauled himself up. He held his hand out to Billy. "Give me a hand out of this thing," he said.

"Rita tried to throw Bertie's relish out," I said, climbing down behind Bishopp.

"What'd she want to go and do a thing like that for?"

I would have told him if Bishopp and Bertie weren't around, but all I said was, "Is there a ladies' room here?"

"Hold on there," Bertie said, coming down from the front of the truck. "You don't go in strange restrooms by yourself."

"I remember," I said, waiting for Bertie to catch up.

When we both had washed up, I headed back, but Bertie didn't. She said the truck was uncomfortable and she preferred to sit down under the shade of a tree.

Mack and Bishopp were standing in front of the truck, Billy beside them, their backs to me. I was just about to climb into the back when I heard Mack say something about a baby.

Billy said something I couldn't hear.

"Like I told Pete," Mack said, "it's more than the cards."

Bishopp said something about how, even though Rita should be pitied and he understood she had lost touch with reality, it angered him to hear such inconceivable accusations. "After all, Phoebe is just a child herself."

I inched closer.

Mack kept saying he was sorry. That this wasn't the first time something like this had happened. That he had told us Rita was jealous. That every time he got a crew together to work the kitchen so that he could get a few dollars in his pocket to get them back to Brooklyn, the cards and the drink would start her up. "But this is the worst, accusing me of something like that. I hope the kid never finds out."

Rita must have told him the terrible thing in my future that she wouldn't tell me about.

"I mean, Phoebe having a kid. My kid —"

I couldn't believe my ears. Me? Having a baby? That's what Rita saw? Chills ran through me. How could that be? Then I thought about what I learned in Sunday school about the Blessed Mother.

"Our Blessed Lady, the Virgin Mary, Mother of God, was visited by an angel while she slept. One sent from God," Louise Longworth's mother said. " 'Mary,' the angel said, 'you are to bring forth a son and you shall call him Jesus.' "

Mrs. Longworth had smiled her Sunday school teacher smile. "It was a miracle, my dear boys and girls. God's son in our Blessed Lady's womb."

One of the boys asked her about Joseph, and wasn't he the father. She'd looked up at the clock, said time was running out, and dismissed the boys.

After the door was closed behind the last of them, she asked the girls to assemble around her desk. "My dears," she said, her voice barely above a whisper, "Mary knew not man." She'd looked around as though the angel were hovering above us. "Remember, girls, there is only one Blessed Lady. One Virgin Mother."

Then she reminded us how Sally June Wickham

had to leave school in the middle of eighth grade to live at Rosemary Hall until she had her baby. "We don't need any more of that kind of goings on, now do we?" We all shook our heads. "And certainly we don't want to shame our good and decent families. It is not God's plan for us."

Bishopp's voice brought me back.

"We're stranded," he said. "We're finished."

"Maybe we can find somebody else to fix the car," Billy said.

"There's nobody other than this guy," Mack said, shaking his head. "And if he said it would take a month of Sundays to get the parts, he should have told you it'd take a year of Sundays for him to fix it."

"This is too much for me," Bishopp said, sighing. "With no place to stay, a car that probably will take more money than we have to fix it, we might as well give up right now."

My heart pounded in my throat. Bertie was right. Prayers fervently said *do* go right to God's ears. We were turning back. We were going home.

❧   ❧   ❧

"But you said we were going home!" I shouted at Bishopp. "I heard you say that."

"Calm yourself," he said. "I did not say that."

"You did. You said we had no car and no place to stay and no money and that you were giving up."

He tried to put his arm around me, but I pulled away. "Sometimes one says things one doesn't necessarily mean when one is upset."

He tried again to reach out to me, but again I pulled away.

He took me by the shoulders. His face was flushed, his hair still standing on end. "You are going to listen to me. Whether I like it or not, we are continuing on this journey. And whether you like it or not, you are going to cooperate.

"Mack has been kind enough to offer the use of one of his trucks. Kind enough to pay us more than we have earned."

"That's only because Rita threw us out."

"She's not responsible for her actions, and Mack isn't responsible for the effect her actions have upon us. He is a good and generous man, Phoebe."

I tried to pull away, but he tightened his grip.

"Listen to me," Bishopp said in a voice he'd never used to me before. "Do you think I want this? Do you think I or Bertie at our age, or Billy, for that matter, want to travel in a truck?"

Again I tried to pull away

His grip tightened. "You are going to hear me out. Do you think this is enjoyable for any of us —"

"I'm not leaving Gram's car here. I want to go back."

"Aaah," he said, nodding, "you're taking over." He dropped his hands to his sides. "Refuse Mack's offer, if that's what you want. Ask the proprietor of this fine establishment if he needs help pumping gas. Whatever." He looked over to where Bertie and Billy stood. "We're willing, correct?"

They didn't answer.

Bishopp looked back at me. "Perhaps you can arrange to set up the car as our sleeping quarters. Or perhaps the woods would be better." He laughed a bitter laugh. "As far as eating is concerned," he said, throwing up his hands, "we won't."

My throat felt as though somebody had stuffed it with rocks. My eyes burned.

"Well?" Bishopp said, his voice hoarse. "I'm waiting for you to tell me what your plans are. You're in charge."

He shook me. "Tell me."

I looked away.

He took my chin in his hand and forced me to face him. "Look at me," he said.

And when I did, he said, his voice low, "Do you think I want to leave your grandmother's car? Do you think I ultimately want to leave —" He dropped his hand, smoothed his hair, and walked away.

I tried hard to stop a sob, but couldn't.

Bishopp turned back. "When one is in charge, there is simply no time for that." Then he headed into the woods behind the gas station.

I looked over at Bertie, then Billy. Billy looked away from me and walked toward Mack, who was sitting by the truck.

Bertie wouldn't look at me; her eyes followed Bishopp. "That man is killing himself, sure as I'm standing here."

Part of me wanted to run after Bishopp to tell him

I didn't want to take charge, to tell him I was sorry, but part of me wouldn't let my feet move from where I stood. Instead they led me to Gram's old car. I got into the backseat and put my head back. My mind raced. I thought about what Bishopp said. And then what Mack said. A baby. The baby Rita kept seeing in the cards. Could it be true? The cards had been right about everything else. But how did it happen? I wanted to go home. But the thought of having to live at Rosemary Hall frightened me. I thought about going to my father. That frightened me, too. He never wanted me, and now what if there was a baby, too?

I thought about the day Mrs. Longworth had told us about the Blessed Mother. Then I thought about Sally June Wickham. "That one," everybody called her. Now maybe I was going to be "that one." I started to cry again. Louise had told me that Sally June let boys touch her "in a certain way." And that when you let boys do that, something happens, and sometimes God sends a baby. Mack had hugged me and kissed me and told me he'd like a kid just like me. "Oh, God," I said, "please help me."

What would I tell Bishopp and Bertie and Billy? Then I remembered what else Louise had said about Sally June. Sally June had tried to keep it a secret, and when everybody found out, her whole family was disgraced.

I hated secrets. I couldn't keep them. But I'd have to keep this one. I felt trapped, and my head pounded. I *had* to do what Gram wanted. Just go along with Bishopp and Bertie, hoping that God would listen and let Bishopp, my own Bishopp, be with me forever. Whatever happened.

I climbed out of the car and asked Billy for the keys to the trunk. One by one, I gathered the boxes filled with Gram's silver, brought them over to Mack's truck, and put them in the back. When I'd finished, I walked to where Bishopp stood, slipped my hand into his, and said, "It's time to go."

And the Lord Takes the Wheel

23

*I*t was as though nothing had changed. Everybody treated me the way they had always treated me. Bishopp thanked me for cooperating and then asked me to help Bertie get the rest of our things out of the trunk. "We should be on the road as soon as possible," he said. "Take advantage of daylight."

I swung the last suitcase into the truck and waited for Bishopp to tell us we were all set to leave.

Leaving wasn't easy. Especially for Bishopp.

Billy had left his prosthesis back at Rita's. His stump had been getting sore and he'd taken to removing it and leaving it in the small room behind the kitchen. Even with it, Billy wasn't sure he was going to be able to manage the controls. "All the gizmos are on the right," he said when Mack tried to show him how to drive the truck. "I'm used to having them on the left with my good arm."

Mack offered to go back to pick up Billy's prosthesis, but when he came back he was empty-handed. Seems it had disappeared, and when Mack asked Rita about it, she told him she didn't know what he was talking about.

Bishopp had no choice. He was to drive the truck.

The owner of the gas station let him practice in the parking lot. Bertie and I sat under a tree and watched.

It was terrible. Every time he came out of the truck after driving around, he'd tell us that Americans drove on the wrong side of the road. "It didn't matter when I was in the passenger seat," he said. "But being the driver is quite another story."

"Left side, right side, wrong side. What's the difference?" Mack said the last time Bishopp got out of the truck.

Bishopp said there was a vast difference and that if Mack thought he knew so much, he ought to take a trip abroad and find out for himself.

Mack paid no attention. "You gotta at least know how to start it before it gets dark," Mack said. "Get in and try again."

Bishopp did, but every time he turned the ignition on, the truck would lurch forward and stall.

"You gotta tell him to put his foot on the clutch at the same time he starts her up," Mack yelled in to Billy, who was sitting beside Bishopp.

"What d'ya think I've been doing?"

"Well, it don't look that way."

Bertie shook her head. "This is too much for him. You forgetting he's no kid?"

I didn't want to be reminded of that.

"Don't you worry about him," Mack said. "You

forgetting how fast he learned to wait on tables? He just needs a little practice."

Mack was wrong. Bishopp needed a lot of practice.

When he finally learned how to start the truck, it was almost dark. Mack got the owner of the gas station to turn on the two dim lights in his parking lot. "This way we'll kill two birds with one stone," Mack called in to Bishopp. "You learn how to handle this baby and you learn how to drive at night."

"I hope we're not the two birds!" Billy called out.

From inside the truck, I could hear Billy telling him to make a right turn.

The truck went around in circles.

"I said right."

Again the truck went around.

"Get him to make a left," Mack yelled.

The truck turned and went around the other way. In circles.

After a long while, Bishopp stopped the truck and got out. "The truck refuses to cooperate."

"That's because you won't let go of the steering wheel," Billy said, jumping down from where he sat. "Once you make the turn, you got to let it slide through your hands so the wheels will straighten out." He put his arm around Bishopp. "Come on, you're doing great."

Things got better after that. Bishopp drove the truck back and forth across the parking lot. After a while, Billy got out of the truck and stood with Mack. "Left. Right. Stop," Mack or Billy would yell.

After a million lefts and rights and stops, Bishopp poked his head out of the window. "How's that for an old English Lord?" he shouted, grinning from ear to ear.

When Bertie was convinced that Bishopp was ready to go out on the road, it was agreed that we would drive Mack back to the restaurant. Bishopp parked in the lot across the road, where Mack said it would be safe for us to spend the night. "Too late for you to travel," he said.

He asked Billy to wait in the shadows outside the restaurant while he went inside to get some things we might need.

When he came back, Mack had mats and blankets and pillows and a canvas cover for the back of the truck. And food. He told us how sorry he was that we were leaving. "It was good having you."

He hugged Bertie when she gave him the recipe for her relish. "This'll make me a million."

Bertie laughed and said she hoped that would take care of getting them back to Brooklyn.

He patted the hood of his truck. "You take good care of her, Pete." He winked over at me. "I'll take good care of your granny's car." He shook hands with Billy and Bishopp and kissed Bertie. I sat very still in the corner of the truck.

We thanked him, but all he said was, "Por nada."

He wished us all good luck and then came over to where I sat. "You take care of yourself, you hear? You're a very special little lady." He leaned in to kiss me good-bye, but I backed away. "Gettin' bashful with old Mack, are you?" He blew me a kiss, then rubbed his hand over his head, pointed to the bumps he'd told me about when we first came, and said, "Take it from me, kid. Fortune-tellin' is for the birds."

PART THREE

&

August 1977:
The Long and Winding Road

Roll On

24

*W*e settled down as soon as Mack left. He had asked us to leave before dawn so that there would be little chance of Rita's seeing the truck with all of us in it. Billy stretched out across the seats in the front, the rest of us in the back. Bishopp and Bertie fell asleep quickly.

It had been a long, hot day. Even now the air was thick. Motionless. Streaks of lightning lit up the August sky, but there was no thunder. No rain to cool down the night. The only sound came from Bertie and Bishopp. Bertie's soft, "put, put, put," Bishopp's "ccnncc, ccnncc, ccnncc," the sound he made only when he was very tired and snored.

I settled myself in the corner of the truck and looked over at Rita's. We'd been there for less than a week, but it seemed much longer. Up in that attic room, all of us together, I really began to believe that that's the way it was going to be. But what the cards told Rita ruined everything.

I tried hard to believe that the cards were just dumb

old cards, as dumb as the bumps on Mack's head, and the baby that kept floating around wasn't a baby but a bunch of kittens. But I couldn't forget the day Rita went over to say good morning to Mack and, just like the cards said, trouble started. Or the day we came and the cards told her all about us. Where we were going and that we had money troubles. That Bertie had never been married. The cards even knew about the letters.

I thought about the letters, especially the one where my father said he would do anything for Gram, because my mother was her daughter, and I was her granddaughter. If he really meant that, maybe he'd do anything for me, even now. But people change.

That's what Billy kept saying I should do. He told me I kept bucking the wind. That I should stop fighting myself, stop wishing for things to be the way I thought they should be. He told me about when he lost his arm. How he woke up and wiggled fingers that weren't there and when a nurse told him it was just a reaction, he'd cried.

"Not for long, though. I thought of some of my buddies who got blown away. Not just an arm. All of them. Gone. Like I say, Phoeb, everybody loses something."

Then he gave me a poke with his stump and said, "Lighten up, girl. Stop carrying that sack of rocks my sister keeps talking about."

How could I lighten up now? How could I stop having a baby? A baby was more than a sack of rocks.

I thought of the movie about the lady who was

having a baby in the midst of the Civil War. How everybody was afraid to help her. How she'd had to travel in an old wagon right after she had the baby. How she almost died. I prayed hard to God that He'd help me. Help me know what to do. I had never even baby-sat a baby. Never held one.

Maybe Mack would want the baby. But what about Rita? Would everybody hate me? Bishopp? My father?

A truck roared past us. I could feel the ground shake beneath us, but nobody stirred.

I didn't want to think anymore. I wiggled down on the mat Mack had given us, plumped up my pillow, and even though I thought I wouldn't sleep, I did.

❧ ❧ ❧

"You old fool, you almost killed me!" somebody yelled.

I sat up and rubbed my eyes, not sure of where I was. The truck looked different, and then I realized somebody had put on the cover Mack had given us. Billy and Bertie had shifted places.

"Morning, Phoeb," Billy said. "You sleep okay?"

I nodded. "Where are we?"

"Heading for South Carolina. You hungry?"

"No." I definitely wasn't hungry. The truck was bouncing and so was my stomach.

"You feeling sick or something?"

I shook my head and lifted up the plastic flap on my side. All I could see for miles were open fields dotted with scrawny pine trees, and I knew Bishopp hadn't convinced Bertie to ride the parkways. He'd tried convincing her just before they fell asleep last night, telling her it would make it easier for him. "Not so many traffic lights to deal with."

But she told him the same thing she'd told Billy. "Not unless the Lord himself is at the wheel."

"You sure you feel okay?" Billy said when I refused the peach he held out to me.

I nodded. "When do you think we'll be leaving Georgia?"

" 'Bout noon," he said, wiping peach juice from his chin.

"We going to stop before that?"

"Soon as we spot some place Bish thinks is big enough for him to maneuver the truck into." He bit into another peach. "I got to give him credit, though. I would have lost it if I had people hollering at me the way they've been hollering at him."

The truck swerved from one lane to another. "You moron!" another somebody yelled. "You're gonna kill someone."

"He is," Billy yelled back. "Us."

We were going slow, so slow I could almost reach out to pick the pinecones that hung from some of the trees. Every time we passed a town, Billy would say, "Don't blink, Phoeb, or you'll miss seeing Jesup," or Hephzibah, or whatever.

He teased Bishopp about looking for an airstrip so he could park the truck, because every time we came to a rest area, Bishopp would say the road leading in was too narrow, or too steep. "I hear they got a big one just outside of Virginia."

"You just keep quiet back there," Bertie said. "He's doing just fine."

Bishopp finally spotted a rest area he could get the truck in and out of without too much trouble. Billy opened the rear and we hopped down.

"You did good," Billy said.

"Good or bad, I was not about to have to rely on a tow truck to get us out."

"I meant what I said. Only took you three tries."

"You stop your wise-guying," Bertie said, holding her hand out, "and help me on down from this old thing."

Ever since we'd left Rita's, and even before, Bertie had been acting a little strange, kind of siding with Bishopp most times. Defending him when Mack or Billy got to teasing him. Back home, they'd never agreed on anything.

As always, Bertie spread out the food and, as always, we all sat down, said a prayer, and ate. It was so strange, all of us doing what we always did, as though nothing had happened. As though I were still the same old Phoebe.

"You want some biscuits, sugar babe?"

"No thanks."

"How about you, Bish?"

"Thank you, Bertie, I think I will."

"Pass the margarine, Phoeb."

"Stop playing with the margarine, little brother, and help us clear up. We're about ready to go."

But before we did, I picked up a rock. I held it in my hand until I saw the sign that said, YOU ARE LEAVING GEORGIA. THANKS FOR COMING AND HURRY BACK. Then I squeezed it hard, so hard it left angry red marks on the palm of my hand.

Lord, You Gave Me a Mountain

25

"Come on, Phoebe, don't be a sourpuss. Sing."

I didn't feel like singing. And I didn't feel like listening to the rest of them sing. They were having such a good time, I couldn't believe it. Like nothing had happened.

It was the same the night before. We'd stopped at a small motel off the road. Bertie kept saying how clean and attractive it was, but it was just a room. Nothing like our room at Rita's.

There was a small restaurant in the lobby where we had our supper. Just before we finished, I thought Bishopp was going to say something about me and this baby, but all he said was that I shouldn't forget to take my motion sickness pill. "We'll be driving straight through tomorrow."

And now, every town we came to, somebody would make up words to "You Are My Sunshine," singing the town's name instead of "Sunshine."

"Listen to this," Billy said when we passed Smoke

Rise, North Carolina. "You are my Smoke Rise, my only Smoke Rise. You keep me comfy when it gets cold. You warm the tootsies on my footsies, keep that smo-o-oke rising my way."

He almost fell out of the truck, he laughed so hard. So did Bertie. Bishopp, too.

He nudged me. "You know what I'm going to sing when we get to Okawala?"

I told him I didn't care, but he went ahead anyway.

"I'm changing the tune on you, Phoeb. Going to sing this one to the tune of 'Oklahoma.' You ready?"

I didn't answer.

"Well, I am. Ohhh, Okawala where the rain keeps beating on your head. Where them little bugs, they don't give hugs, 'cause they're busy biting your —" He nudged me again.

"Quit it, Billy."

"— 'cause they're busy biting your behind." Again, he nudged me.

"I said to quit it."

Billy shook his head. "I'm telling you, Phoeb, sometimes you act like a fifty-year-old lady instead of a kid."

"And you act about five."

He laughed and sang another chorus of "Okawala." "What'd you think of that?" he said, giving me a push.

"I think it's stupid, and quit pushing at me."

"I take back what I said about you being like a

fifty-year-old lady. You're more like one who's ninety." He gave me one last push.

"Stop it!" I punched his good arm. I punched it again. And again. Billy didn't move, he just kind of smiled.

"I'm sorry this one didn't get blown off, too," I yelled. As soon as I said it, I was sorry.

The smile left Billy's face.

"I'm sorry, Billy."

He didn't answer me.

"Did you hear me?"

He turned and looked away. I walked on my knees over to him. "I'm sorry, Billy. I'm really sorry." I sat next to him. "It wasn't your singing." I reached out and put my hand on his stump. He flinched, but didn't pull away. "I don't want to go to my father. I don't want to leave all of you." My voice got louder. "I'm scared. Scared of everything. Scared of having a baby —"

He looked at me, puzzled. "What are you talking about?"

"A baby!" I screamed. The floodgates of hysteria opened up and, once started, wouldn't stop.

"I'm having a baby," I wailed.

The truck lurched and stopped, then lurched again, skidded and bounced until it came to a final stop.

As soon as Billy's feet hit the ground, Bishopp and Bertie were beside him.

Even in my state of hysteria, I could see the expressions on their faces. All the same: horrified.

Confession

26

They waited until I calmed down, their faces frozen in the same expression as when I had climbed down from the truck.

"What is this all about?" Bishopp asked. "Surely I didn't hear correctly. Surely this must be your imagination. You know how vividly you can imagine things."

"It's true. You knew . . ."

"I knew?" he said, his face as colorless as ice. He turned to Bertie. "This has to be a dream. A nightmare she's had."

I shook my head. "Rita knew . . ." A sob took over. "She knew . . ."

"About what?" Bishopp asked.

"Tell me, Phoebe" he said, gently. "Please tell me."

"About . . . about . . . the baby . . . the cards said . . ."

"Those damn cards," Billy said.

Bertie shushed him.

Bishopp took a deep breath and put his hand on mine. "Phoebe, dear, the cards are meaningless. Poppycock. Rita is disturbed —"

"She's not. Mack knew, too. He said he hoped . . . he said he hoped, I'd never know what Rita had said about the kid. His kid."

Bertie handed me a towel and I wiped my face.

"You were there when he said that," I said, looking at Bishopp.

"How could something like this happen?" Bishopp asked no one in particular.

"God," I said, sitting down in the grass. "God made it happen."

Bertie told Billy to take Bishopp for a little walk. Then she sat down beside me. "Phoebe," she said, after she settled herself, "tell Bertie what you're thinking. All that you're thinking."

"That I'm having a baby."

"Tell me why you think that."

"Because of what Louise told me about Sally June Wickham. How she let boys touch her in a certain way. How when you do that something happens and sometimes God sends you a baby."

"Go on."

I told her how Rita had said there was a baby floating around every time she read my cards. How she'd said maybe it was mine. How she'd put me out, telling me that there was something wrong, that she couldn't tell me. How Mack had hugged me and kissed the top of my head. How he'd told me he'd like to have a kid just like me.

Bertie reached over and hugged me. "Oh, my sweet baby. I'm sorry. Very sorry. This is my doing. Trying so hard to do what's right and forgetting you were growing up and needing to know things."

She rocked me back and forth. "This is why you need your daddy, a real parent —"

"He won't want me now."

She put me at arm's length. "You listen to me. There's no baby —"

"But —"

"No, child. Louise was wrong. More's got to happen between a man and a woman."

Then she told me, made me understand how people who love one another come together, penis to vagina. How when a man truly loves a woman, and the woman truly loves him back, that something does happen that is wonderful. "And sometimes, in His wisdom, God sends them a child. Like you, Phoebe. Part your mother. Part your father."

I asked her to tell me about him, and for the first time she did. "He was with us for such a short while, but it was good. He loved your momma, and she loved him. You've got his dark eyes, Phoebe." She took my hand in hers. "And you've got his long, bony fingers." She laughed a little. "Your grandmother always said he looked like a young Abe Lincoln. He did. But he was better looking. Softer."

I asked her why my grandmother forbade them to speak of him. "She was hurt and angry that he'd left your momma, her being pregnant and all. She forgot it was your momma who made him go. She was a sweet one, your momma. She wanted him to have a chance to do what he wanted. But when she died, your grandma, all of us, forgot that. All we remembered is that he left. Nobody cared if we ever saw him again." She hugged me. "But time changes most people. Even your grandma."

I shuddered. "Bertie, I did something terrible. I found Gram's papers. I lied to Bishopp so he wouldn't know where my father is."

"Oh, sugar babe, he knows where your daddy is. He didn't need to see those papers to know that. Your grandma remembered. He knew from the start where we needed to go." She hugged me hard. "And he knows that you need to keep that letter to yourself."

I pulled away from her. "He saw it?"

She nodded. "When Rita threw everything out the window." She laughed, her arm around me again. "Bishopp's pretty quick on his feet."

I kind of shook my head. "I guess so . . ." Then I smiled, too, thinking about how I'd raced Bishopp to get at them. "Real quick."

I got serious again. "Do you think my father will love me, Bertie?"

"If he doesn't, sweet thing, he's made out of stone.

"You stop your worrying and help me up from

here." She held her hands out to me. "Give Bertie the old heave-ho."

I stood before her and took her hands. "I'm going to miss you," I said.

Her eyes filled up. "Doing what's right sure doesn't make you feel good." She sighed a long sigh. "What's right is for you to be with your daddy. I know that, but —" She dropped her hands and her body shook with sobs. I got down beside her and put my arms around her. I rocked her back and forth as she'd done with me so many times before. I smoothed her hair and told her how much I loved her. How much I'd always love her. My body shook, too, and the tears came, but I kept holding her.

After a long while, she stopped crying, and said, "Come on, Phoebe, get on up and give Bertie the old heave-ho."

When we were up on our feet, she squeezed my hands and said, "Nobody does it like you do."

When Bishopp and Billy came back, Bertie told them that things had been taken care of. She asked Billy to get the picnic hamper out. Seeing it was almost noon, and the day so nice, we could have an early dinner.

I never loved Bertie and Billy and Bishopp as much as I loved them that day. Not one of them made me feel silly for thinking I was having a baby. Not one of them joked about it, or laughed, or ever talked about it again.

Song Sung Blue

27

*B*ishopp surprised all of us. He had gotten to be a pretty good driver. Almost a day had passed and nobody had yelled out to him. I surprised me, too. I got to enjoying the songs Billy made up. We sang at the top of our lungs when we came into a town, especially one called Hortense. Billy dedicated it to the girl he had taken to his high school prom, Hortense Miller.

But Bertie was the one that really surprised us. The night before, she'd tried to call Ginny Graham to let her know when we'd be arriving, but got no answer. All morning Bertie asked Bishopp to pull over whenever she spotted a telephone.

"Something's wrong," she said, as she climbed back into the truck after making the last phone call. "Henry must be bad off."

She got back into her seat next to Bishopp and we started off again.

Billy and I stopped singing. Bishopp tried to comfort Bertie, telling her there were many reasons people don't answer telephones, and it didn't necessarily mean that something was wrong.

Bertie said nothing. We drove on, quiet except for an occasional outburst from Billy. "Coming into Phinizy. Population fifty-two."

We stopped at about nine to have some breakfast, and just as we were about to climb back into the truck, Bertie made her announcement.

"Something's wrong, I feel it." She turned to Bishopp. "How many days have we got to go?"

'The way we've been going, we'll be there day after tomorrow."

"If we took the highways?"

"You mean the Lord agreed to drive?" Billy said, laughing.

I laughed, too, but one look from Bertie stopped me, as it did Billy.

"Late tomorrow, if we drive most of the day," Bishopp said. "I hesitate to push this truck beyond a certain speed."

Bertie took a deep breath. "I'm feeling real uneasy. I think we should take the highway."

Billy started to climb in the back of the truck, but Bertie asked him to sit up with Bishopp. "I'll go in the back," she said. "That way I won't see what's coming."

Bertie hated the back. The mats served as seats and faced the rear, and sitting under the canvas cover with its plastic ventilation flaps was confining and hot. She settled herself down, then turned to me and, her voice low, said, "Ginny needs me, sugar babe."

I knew that, but it was still hard to let go. I looked over at her, really looked at her: legs stretched out on the metal floor of the truck, feet puffy from the heat, sweat trickling down her face, arms crossed over her chest.

I thought about a movie we had seen at Shady Lawn about a family who travels to California in a truck. "Okies," Billy had told me. "People trying to get to a better place." It was sad, so sad Bertie and I left before it was over. "Too painful for me to watch," Bertie had said. "I don't think they're going to make it."

I reached out to Bertie. "It's okay," I said. "Besides, we'll be coming down to visit. You'll be coming up to visit us. It's not like we won't see each other."

She smiled at me. "That's right," she said.

Billy started to sing again as we passed another town. I forced myself to join in; so did Bertie. When we finished the last chorus, Bertie took my hand and kissed it. "My baby's growing up," she said. "Fast."

Where Have All the Good Times Gone?

28

The night before we'd stayed at a small motel off the road. We had supper and got ready for bed early. Nobody said very much.

When everybody was asleep, I got out of bed and sat by the window. There was no moon, no stars, and I was as lonely as the night we'd all slept in the car. I remembered how I'd snuggled up against Bertie's warm body and counted the sounds of the night. But now everything was different. There would be no more nights with just the four of us. Together.

"Hey, Phoeb," Billy called back. "Come back to life." He pointed to a sign that read: WELCOME TO VIRGINIA. DRIVE CAREFULLY. "We made it," he said. "We're almost there."

When we passed the sign that welcomed us to Virginia, I curled up and willed myself to sleep. I didn't wake up until we were at Ginny Graham's house.

Bertie was right. There was something very wrong at Ginny Graham's. A big black ribbon hung from her door, and even though there was little late-afternoon sun, the shades were drawn in every window.

Henry Graham had died the day we left Lubelle County. There had been no way for Ginny to get in touch with Bertie. She had waited for Bertie to call, but when days turned into a week, she buried Mr. Graham in the cemetery behind the churchyard and went into mourning.

That's the way Bertie found her, sitting in her darkened living room, the only light coming from the tiny window over the fireplace. Ginny's neighbor told Bertie that Ginny hadn't cried since Henry died.

When Ginny saw Bertie, it was as though she had been waiting for her to hold on to, so she could cry without shattering into tiny pieces.

Bertie held her for a long time, telling her how sorry she was that she hadn't been there. When Ginny had cried herself out, Bertie put her to bed, then came out to the kitchen and fixed us something to eat.

After saying a prayer, we ate quickly, cleaned up the kitchen, and settled ourselves in Ginny's tiny parlor. Billy sat in Ginny's old rocking chair, his legs spread, his eyes closed. Bertie sat dozing, Bishopp beside her, their heads drooping to their chests. The silence that had been with us the night before filled every corner. The clock on Ginny's wall ticked.

After everybody had settled down for the night, I lay on Ginny Graham's sofa, the clock tick, ticking away, and tried to sleep. But my head felt like a giant balloon as thoughts came in and wouldn't leave. Bishopp and I would be leaving in the morning, and in a day or so we'd be in Maine. And then what?

Bertie had been right about Ginny needing her. It was strange how people sometimes knew what was going to happen. Bertie did. Rita, too. Even though she was wrong about the baby, she could have been right about the terrible things she couldn't tell me. Things I already knew. It was going to be bad when I got to my father's.

🐦 🐦 🐦

"Phoebe," I heard someone call. "Phoebe."

I opened my eyes and Bishopp was standing over me.

"It's getting quite late. Bertie has breakfast ready."

I dressed quickly and gathered my things together.

Bertie was at the stove, Billy sitting at the table. She didn't turn. "French toast, Phoebe. Your favorite."

"Morning, Phoeb," Billy said.

It was like any other morning. Bertie fixing breakfast. Billy saying good morning. I sat beside him and drank my juice, and when Bertie put the French toast in front of me, I asked Billy to pass the syrup. Just like we'd done so many yesterday mornings.

Billy excused himself and said he was going to help Bishopp load up the truck. Billy had told me the day before that he wouldn't be staying at Ginny's for too long. "I'll help settle things here, then I'm going back to finish up my degree," he'd said. "Always wanted to teach, and now is the time, Phoeb." He'd asked me not to say anything to Bertie. "I want to break it to her gently."

I didn't eat much, and when I was finished I brought the dish over to the sink. Bertie was standing, her back to me, drinking a cup of coffee. "Excuse me, Bertie," I said. "I want to rinse this."

She dropped her cup and turned, put her arms around me, and held me. She didn't say a word. Just held on to me. So tight, I could barely breathe. I bit my lip and held my breath, determined not to cry.

"Ginny says to tell you you're welcome here anytime. You hear?"

"I hear," I said, her warm breast muffling my voice.

"You remember what I told you about hitchhiking?"

"I'll remember."

"I'll come visiting with Billy soon as we get settled." A moan began in her throat and made its way to her lips. "Your daddy's going to love you. You hear me?"

"I hear you." I looked up at her and forced a smile.

"Thank you, Bertie. For everything."

"Anytime you're ready, Phoebe," Bishopp called in from the living room.

Bertie let go of me. "It's right that you should go." She sniffed deeply and took a handkerchief from her pocket. "You go on now."

I kissed her quickly, asked her to say good-bye to

Ginny, and ran out to where Bishopp stood waiting, Billy beside me.

"You take care," Billy said, helping me up to the passenger's seat.

I nodded, afraid to trust my voice.

He shut the door, then reached in and squeezed my arm lightly. "You ever need me, Phoeb, you know where I am."

I nodded, looking straight ahead.

"You take care, too, Bish."

Bishopp started the motor and we were on our way.

I looked in the side mirror at Billy getting smaller and smaller and smaller until he finally disappeared from sight.

Through a Glass Eye

29

*I*t didn't take long for us to get out of Virginia and into Washington, D.C. Into Maryland and on to Pennsylvania. Exit signs with the town names whizzed by. They were just places we passed without Billy to sing about them. It's funny how somebody becomes connected to something forever. How I knew for the rest of my life I'd think of Billy when I saw a sign naming a town. And from somewhere, from where things like that are stored, I'd hear his voice singing about Smoke Rise, and Hortense and all the rest.

I rested my head by the open window, and in the distance I heard church bells. Sundays always made me feel lonely. Gram and the rest loved Sundays, but I didn't. Not because of church, or anything like that. Just the feeling that Sundays brought. Stillness. A stillness that isn't like the stillness of sitting by the river listening to the sound of the water, or coming into Bertie's kitchen before dawn, everyone asleep in the house, to watch the sun slowly light up the darkness. But a stillness that's lonely and empty.

Bishopp made a valiant attempt to cheer me up that lonely Sunday morning. When we passed a town named Funkstown, he sang something about Funkstown making him feel funky, then he rhymed it with hunky, and dunky. I laughed a false laugh, so as not to hurt his feelings, but it made me feel even lonelier and sadder.

Even though Bertie had wanted to fix us both dinner and supper, Bishopp said we'd stop midday at a McDonald's. That was to cheer me up, too, I knew. We had burgers and fries and shakes. At first, conversation came hard. Bishopp commented on how thin the fries were. I agreed. "Bertie's burgers would put these to shame," he said, biting into his. I agreed.

"I might apply for a job here," he said, drinking the last of his shake. "I was getting quite good at Rita's."

"I didn't like it when they called you Pete."

"I know, it's not dignified. But I rather liked it. It becomes tiresome to be called my one's surname all of one's life."

"But you're more Bishopp than you are Pete."

He nodded. "I suppose," he said, gathering up the trash. "Come along," he said, "time to get on the road, Howland Fiore."

For the first time that day, I really laughed.

Bishopp dumped the rubbish into a container, and we were on our way. When we passed the state line into New York, he sang "East Side, West Side." I reluctantly joined him in the last chorus.

At about five o'clock and well into Connecticut, Bishopp began to look for a place to stay.

"Here, Phoebe," he said, passing me the guidebook, "have a look. I'm pretty sure I saw one of those budget places in a town near New London. Westminster, I believe. A bit in from the shore, but it sounded quite good."

He braked for a red light.

"Ipswich," he said, stretching his arms and arching his back. "Back home that was quite a nice place, too."

"Did you ever live there?"

He shook his head. "Too rich for the likes of my family." He put his foot on the gas and we were off again. "We lived in a tiny village outside London. Bainsbridge." He laughed. "That sounds quite nice, too, but in truth, it was a poor little place. But I might well go back there one day. Perhaps visit my sister."

"I thought you didn't like being with her."

He grinned over at me. "True. Felicity is a gloomy creature. She came into this world with her shoulders drooped, and I fear she'll go out the same way. But she's my sister."

A scary thought kept creeping through my head, and it was hard to push it away. Bishopp had said he'd stay with me as long as I needed him. I'd always need him. But would he stay always?

He went on to tell me that Felicity never married and blamed him for that. " 'Had to stay with Mum,' she'd always say."

He retold how he'd left home at fourteen to work for my grandfather Howland, and how, many years

185 ❧

later, my grandmother and Bertie had come into their lives. "Olivia brightened up Mr. Howland's world." How grief stricken my grandmother was when my grandfather died. How she married Mr. Culver Daniels, who proceeded to drain her emotionally and financially. He was just about to tell me about his first encounter with Bertie when he slowed the car down and said, "Aaah, what have we here?"

In a large field, there were all sorts of tents. Flags flew everywhere. In the distance, I heard music, smelled something cooking.

"It's a carnival," Bishopp said, stopping the truck. "How about it, Phoebe? Shall we give it a whirl?"

I wasn't really in the mood, but I was glad for any delay.

We bought popcorn and rode on the rides. I hesitated about going on the Ferris wheel, but Bishopp urged me on.

When the ride was over, we went over to look at a huge glass box, almost like a telephone booth. Inside was a plaster fortune-teller. Her blue glass eyes stared straight at us. She wore beads and bracelets, and a scarf was wrapped around her head. Bishopp put in a dime and waited. The fortune-teller's plaster arms rose and moved over the cards spread before her.

One of her plaster hands touched card after card, and just as she was about to push one toward the opening, the lights went off and her hand froze in midair.

Bishopp laughed and said that all our futures were like that. "Floating around in midair." He tossed some popcorn up high, then kind of circled his head around so some of it landed in his mouth. He munched on the popcorn and passed the bag to me. "It's quite good, Phoebe." But to me it was dry and stuck in my throat.

"Let's go see the clowns," Bishopp said. "I've always loved them." I didn't, but we found seats and settled back. I thought about the plaster fortune-teller, how the lights went off just as she was going to give Bishopp the card telling his fortune. Just like Rita had done to me.

"Cotton candy here," a vendor called out. "Peanuts. Cracker Jacks."

Bishopp passed me a huge cotton candy and took one for himself. It seemed so strange to see him bite into the sugary web. "I've never eaten this before," he said, smiling at me, his lips red where the pink candy had touched.

He was different somehow. Back home I knew him, all of him. But now there were parts of him, like there were parts of me, I didn't know or understand.

The clowns came out jumping and flipping and falling. Bishopp laughed so hard, he hiccuped. I thought they were silly and turned and watched the aerialists. They swung back and forth on their trapeze swings, leapt to the catcher, back to the swing, then back to the platform.

There was a drumroll and the ringmaster asked for the audience's attention. "What you are about to witness is a death-defying, never-before-performed act," he announced, spinning around in the ring, bowing to each section he faced. "First Roberto will do a double-double — a double somersault combined with a double twist — the most difficult trick ever invented. And then . . . and then," he went on, "Arturo will do the impossible. He will do a triple somersault, blindfolded. Alberto will catch." He held up his hands to quiet everybody. "I must ask for complete silence."

A soft drumroll began. Roberto stood on the platform, motionless, then leapt to the swing. He flew from the swing, flipping his body over and over, and then from nowhere, Alberto was there to catch him. The audience cheered. The ringmaster asked for quiet again. The soft drumroll began, and Arturo took his place on the platform, blindfolded.

I put my hands over my eyes, afraid to watch. I peered through one finger to see Arturo fly through the air to the swing. Then he somersaulted three times before reaching out to Alberto, who was there for him. The band played. The audience stamped and cheered. And somebody hit Bishopp on the head with a roll of toilet tissue.

It was one of the clowns. It was part of his act. He threw the rolls into the audience, and the audience would throw them back, knocking him to the ground. But if a roll hit somebody, that somebody had to help the clown finish up his act.

Without hesitating, Bishopp got up and went down to the ring. The audience clapped for him. Bishopp took a big bow. Bishopp's job was to round up the toilet tissue. The clown held a huge blower. He had

Bishopp hold the tissue to the blower, and it unrolled until the sheets billowed above them like a big cloud. The clown took Bishopp's hand and they danced underneath. Suddenly the blower turned off and the tissue fell on top of them. The audience cheered. I cringed. When Bishopp had disentangled himself from the mess, he shook hands with the clown, bowed to the howls of the audience, then came and sat down.

"What did you think of that?"

Before I could answer he said, "I might go to clown school." He laughed and then said it was about time we were on our way.

And that part of me that knew Bishopp wouldn't be with me forever took over most of me. The little part that was left felt as though it was suffocating.

The day turned into evening, and when we'd settled into the motel Bishopp had found, we went out to get something to eat.

"They call supper 'dinner' here," he said looking up at the waitress.

She nodded.

"It would make it more universal if we all called it 'dupper.'"

She smiled a weak smile and asked for our orders.

When the food came, I couldn't eat. I was thinking about the day to come, our last day together. Really together. I wanted to do what I had done when I was little and somebody had refused me something — flee from the house, run until I couldn't breathe, sit under a tree till I was sure everybody would be worrying about me. Only then I'd return to find nobody had been worried. Nobody was searching. Police hadn't been called. Gram would be playing Bosendorfer. Bishopp would be adjusting his telescope. Bertie would be on the porch. Billy off somewhere.

I'd feel so alone, but never as alone as I felt now.

"Phoebe, you've eaten nothing."

My throat tightened. I got up, walked quickly out the door, and climbed into the truck.

Bishopp was beside me before I got the door closed.

He put his arm around me.

"You're going to leave me, too," I said, my voice barely above a whisper, my heart pounding in my throat. I looked up at him. "Aren't you?"

He nodded. "In time, I'll leave physically," he said. "But Phoebe, people don't have to be in one another's physical presence to be with them. Is Bertie any less Bertie because she's not sitting here with us? Or Billy? Or your grandmother? Not to me, Phoebe." He pulled me closer. "And that's how it will be with us."

"I'm afraid," I said. "I don't want to go to my father. He won't want me. I know it. Not because of what Rita said. It's what I know. He never wanted me. How could he want me now?" I dug my nails into my knees to stop the tears I knew were coming. "He said he could only love my mother. Bertie once told me there are people like that. And you once told me that your father never loved anybody." I took a deep breath, trying to control myself. "He'll be like that, too. I know it. He will. And you'll be gone." I turned toward the window. "Please, please, take me with you. Take me home."

Bishopp waited for a long while before he spoke, and when he did, he talked very softly.

"Phoebe, I have something to tell you, and I would ask that you hear me out." He took his arm from me, put both hands on the wheel of the truck, and looked straight ahead. "When your mother died, your grandmother was distraught. Her daughter was gone, your father was off playing in some kind of group, her career had faded into nothing. All she had was you."

He looked at me briefly and said, "Try to think of that when I tell you the rest." He sighed a long sigh.

"Phoebe, your father never knew of your existence."

"I don't understand —"

"Your grandmother kept you a secret."

"That's not true —"

"It *is* true. Beyond a doubt. Do you remember the day we searched for the papers that you'd already found, and I went to visit your grandmother?" He didn't wait for an answer. "She was almost like her old self that day. I believe she willed herself to be. She told me that when your father came to visit her, and this I remember myself, she sent Bertie off to visit Ginny Graham and me off to England for a holiday. She packaged you up and sent you off with Miss Jean, because she had led your father to believe there *was* no baby. That you had died along with your mother."

I shook my head. "She wouldn't do that."

"She would and she did."

He turned to me again. "Those papers you found, the ones you wanted so desperately to keep from me. What do you think your father meant when he said the end came so quickly? He meant his wife *and* baby had died.

"All these years, your grandmother forbade Bertie or me to be in touch with him. 'He doesn't want any part of her. He's not fit to care for a child.' We honored her wishes then."

"Why would she do that to me? Why?"

"She was afraid she'd lose you."

My heart was pounding. My breath came fast. I felt as though I were in a blender and somebody had turned the motor on, and I was swirling around, not able to stop.

"Listen to me, Phoebe," he said, his voice gentle.

I shook my head.

"Your father knows of you now."

I turned and faced him, and even though my heart was pounding in my ears, I heard what he said.

"I've been in touch with him. As Bertie told you, your grandmother remembered." He put his hand on mine. "He's waiting for you."

I shivered, thinking of my father, a stranger, getting a call from a stranger telling him another stranger was coming to live with him. It was like a movie. One that had never been made, because nobody would believe it. Even me.

Bridge over Troubled Waters

30

*M*orning came quickly. I'd tossed and turned most of the night, and when I finally fell asleep I dreamed the dream I often had. But this time even Bishopp was gone.

> *I am in that same field, alone, millions of yellow dandelions in bloom, my father waiting at the same clearing. I try to cross the field, but, again, the dandelions turn into great balls of seeds. A cold wind comes and whirls the silvery seeds around and around, blinding me. I call out to my father, but he just stands there, watching. I cry out again and again, until my body crumples onto the grass, resigned.*

I screamed so loud Bishopp woke up. He came over to my bed and held me. When I finally calmed down he began to talk about the carnival. About the aerialist who chose to be blindfolded. "Imagine," he said, "flying through the air blindfolded."

"It was just a circus act," I said.

He shook his head. "It was more than a circus act, Phoebe. Think about it. That man trusted the catcher would be there for him. It was an act of faith." He stood up and tucked the blanket around me. "That's what you must do. Trust that somebody will be there to catch you."

When I woke up the next morning, I could hear Bishopp running the water in the tiny bathroom.

"You awake out there?" he called from behind the door.

"How did you know?"

"Aaaah, my pretty one," he said coming out the door, "I read my bumps."

I laughed, remembering what Rita had told Mack about his head bumps.

"Come along, now," he said, when I had washed and dressed, "it's time we get on the road."

The drive from Westminster to Sadler's Island was a long one. Again and again, all along the road, Bishopp told me things would be just fine. Again and again, I tried to believe it.

My stomach was tight, and when I saw the sign welcoming us to Maine, it threw itself into a knot. I tried thinking about Roberto and Arturo. How they trusted without seeing. How people of faith do that. Bertie, for instance.

I thought about Gram and what she had done. I still didn't understand. I would have loved her even if I saw her only once a year. She'd still be my grandmother.

We stopped at a roadside restaurant for breakfast. The day had turned cold, the sun had disappeared. "Good day for some hot tea," Bishopp said.

"How are you doing?" Bishopp asked, helping himself to another muffin, pouring the last of his tea. "You've eaten less than you ate last night. Is it your stomach?"

I shook my head.

He leaned back in his chair. "Your father is a fisherman. Has his own boat.

"Plays the harp with a string group, too.

"I'm glad of that, Phoebe. It would have been a pity for him to give that up. He asked if you played an instrument.

"I told him of course you did. I said, why, Phoebe's the finest flautist in all of Lubelle County.

"He wasn't surprised. Not surprised at all.

"Asked what you looked like, too.

"Tall for almost twelve, and a bit thin, I told him. Lovely brown hair. And soft, brown eyes that she squints a lot."

He leaned over and took my hand. "Phoebe, listen to me. I'm not deserting you. I'm taking you to your father. A father who wants you. Needs you. Give him a chance. He deserves that. Everybody does. Do you understand?"

I nodded. I didn't really understand, but I knew there was no turning back.

"Well," he said, "shall we go?"

"How far is it from here to Sadler's Island?"

"About twenty-five miles."

We rode in silence until we saw the sign that said, "Next Right Turn — Sadler's Island." We left the main road and turned onto a narrow dirt road. The smell of salt air was strong.

When the road became a small bridge that led to the island, Bishopp reached over and took my hand. I clutched his.

The truck rumbled over the wooden span beneath us. And when we came to the end, I let go of his hand and took a deep breath. And another. And yet another.

There was no field. No dandelions, no yellow flowers for me to gather. No clearing. Just sand with sea beyond.

In the distance, I saw a man standing by the side of the road. Waiting. He was tall and very thin, his hair dark.

Bishopp guided the truck toward him, and when we came to a stop, Bishopp again took my hand and squeezed it lightly.

"There he is," Bishopp said.

I looked up at him, panicked.

"I'm not going anywhere," he said. "I'll be here."

I reached down and rummaged through my suitcase until I found what I was looking for. I smoothed the wrinkles from the creamy-white linen jacket. Bishopp's jacket.

Bishopp smiled, then climbed down from the truck and came around to my side. He opened the door and took my hand in his, nodded a nod that said, It's all right, things are going to be fine. Then gently, so gently, he said, "It's time to meet your father."

I stifled a sob. "I love you, Bishopp." Then I kissed him and whispered, "Pete, too."

He hugged me very hard. "And I love you, Phoebe. All of you."

I climbed down from the truck, my shoes sinking into the sand. I crossed my fingers and hoped my prayer had reached God's ear. I stood very still. The sun appeared and I squinted against the bright light.

The man walked toward me, squinting, too. I slipped into Bishopp's jacket, looked back at Bishopp one last time, then turned and took a few steps. When I got closer, I saw tears running down the man's cheeks. He smiled and reached out to me with long, bony fingers.

"Hi, Phoebe," my father said. "Welcome home."